SEXY SHORTS

VOLUME 1

KATHRYN NOLAN

Copyright © 2018 Kathryn Nolan

All Rights Reserved

This is a work of fiction. Names, characters, places, and incidents either are the products of the author's imagination or are used fictitiously. Any resemblance to actual persons, living or dead, businesses, companies, events, or locales is entirely coincidental.

Editing by Faith N. Erline
Cover by Kari March

ISBN: 978-1-945631-57-3 (ebook)
ISBN: 978-1-945631-34-4 (paperback)

123019

CONTENTS

One Hell of a Restaurant	1
Wild Horse	13
The Hero and the Rookie	23
Did You Touch Yourself?	53
The Gift	59
He was Luke Skywalker (not Han Solo)	71
Like Thieves in the Night	79
Ambrose	87
The Wedding	97
Another Boring Night at the Opera	133
Seize the Day	141
She'll always know the truth	147
Let It Be You	153
Cuffed	161
Author's Note	227
Acknowledgments	229
Hang Out With Kathryn!	231
About Kathryn	232
Books By Kathryn	233

*For Jodi, Joyce, and Julia, the original fans of my #SexyShorts.
Thank you for everything.*

ONE HELL OF A
RESTAURANT

*N*athan has taken me to the fanciest restaurant in the city for one reason.

And one reason only.

"Excuse me?" I say, clutching at the pearls I only wear when I'm feeling fancy. Everything in this restaurant sparkles with wealth and a quiet, humming power. I can see my reflection in my champagne glass.

I sip, the bubbles sliding down my throat.

And I say again: "*Excuse me?*"

Nathan grins lazily, the cat caught with the mouse.

"Not much else to say." He strokes the inside of my wrist with his long fingers. "I have a fantasy that involves you. One I've thought about at least once a day, every day, since we started dating."

It's been over a year now, and I still pinch myself, watching him undress each night, muscles rippling beneath his skin. Those full lips. His unbroken, urgent need to touch me. Possess me. Introduce me to a new pleasure so intense it leaves me breathless.

"And you want to do that... here?" I ask, looking around us. We're in the very back of the restaurant—a dimly lit alcove.

"Yes," he says simply before leaning across the table to give me a hard, commanding kiss. His groan vibrates against my lips.

"Please," he says, nipping with his teeth. "Please give this to me."

He is *always* like this. Powerful and dominating. But then, in an instant, begging me to save him.

"Oh... okay," I stumble. I'm nervous, and he can tell. His lips hover over my ear.

"I'm going to slide beneath this tablecloth now. I'm going to kneel in front of you, like the goddamn goddess you are.

And then I'm going to tongue that sweet pussy of yours until you orgasm in front of everyone here."

My eyes flutter closed.

"How will... how will I hide it?"

Nathan pulls back and pins me with a dangerous gaze.

"That sounds like a problem you'll need to figure out, gorgeous."

And then, like a dream, he ducks beneath the cloth and settles himself in front of me. I can feel him, the coiled strength. His breath, hot against my skin. His thumbs, gliding up my inner thighs and pushing them open, not gently. All around me, couples talk. Kiss. Hands, lingering—one long, delicious foreplay. I wonder if they *know*; can they sense what's about to happen to me?

A tug and then the shredded fabric of my underwear drops to the floor. His tongue is *insistent*. Two fingers fucking into me with slow ease. He works magic, knowing just how to tease me. Take me higher. I swallow my moans, hands tight on my champagne flute. Beneath the tablecloth I thread my fingers in his hair and pull him closer, urging him on.

Then I settle back, the queen on her mighty throne. The goddess he loves fiercely and worships like I deserve.

He traces a maddening pattern, fingers stroking deep inside me. I'm about to climax in front of dozens of people enjoying a steak dinner.

They *can't* know I'm about to come. Although a small part of me is desperate for it—for them to watch as I fly apart under his skillful ministrations. My orgasm beckons, and I lay my head on the table, cloth napkin shoved into my mouth. Nathan slips a third finger inside, sucks my clit between his lips. Everything tightens, then explodes, as I scream around the cloth, bucking shamelessly against his mouth. The world narrows to just me and him, and I know, suddenly, that it will always be like this.

Complete and total *ecstasy*.

Nathan nuzzles my hand, pressing a kiss against my palm. I flag down a passing waiter.

"More champagne please," I pant. "I want to congratulate my boyfriend on a job well done."

I'M PRETTY sure I'm watching a beautiful woman orgasm in a restaurant.

"Do you see what I see?" I whisper to Grant, a guy I met on Tinder three dates ago. We have absolutely nothing in common except for white-hot chemistry.

And he's sexy as *sin*.

His eyes slide to the woman sitting by herself in the alcove. Her hand is moving beneath the tablecloth, no date in sight. Grant glides his hand up my thigh. I'm wearing the shortest dress in the world, and his rough fingers on my inner thigh is divine.

"Tell me what you see," he whispers, in a voice like sandpaper. I swallow, already too aware of his lips on the shell of my ear. His hand pushes between my legs.

"Well... I, um, I think her guy is under that table." I spread my legs further as he nuzzles my neck.

"And I think..." The woman is panting now, one hand squeezing the champagne flute so hard it could break. "And I think I'm watching her get eaten out."

Grant rubs my clit in slow, lazy circles. I jump in my chair.

"Shhh," he soothes. "Keep talking."

A waiter asks if we want a dessert menu, and we both shake our heads furiously.

"I think he's on his knees." The woman's head tilts back. "She's... *God,* I think she's going to come in front of us." He rubs my clit harder, and my vision darkens. His teeth graze my shoulder.

"What do you want?" he rumbles.

"To see her orgasm," I say, and almost instantly she does, biting into a napkin, head on the table. Underneath the table, I grab Grant's hand.

"I don't want to stop touching you," he groans.

"Me neither," I say, turning to look at him. I know this won't last more than a few hot, hard fucks. Which is fine by me. Between the stress of the law firm and too-many family obligations, I just want to spend a week drugged out on sexual bliss.

"Meet me in the bathroom," I say, brushing my lips over his. His answering gasp is all that I need. His eyes rake over every inch of my skin as I saunter away, wet and ready. Thinking about that woman—a queen on her throne being serviced like she demands.

Luckily, this fancy-as-fuck restaurant has a gorgeous, private bathroom. I slip inside and barely have time to fluff my hair and check my teeth for food before he's there.

Grant locks the door, slowly undoes his belt, and gives me the kind of look the Wolf must have given Red. I arch an eyebrow. His belt hits the floor.

In an instant, he has me hauled up on the counter, hair pulled savagely. Tears prick my eyes, the pain and pleasure shimmering through me.

"You're the sexiest woman alive," he growls, palming my breasts through my dress, sucking my nipples through the fabric. I bite back a moan... and then don't.

"You want people to hear," he smiles, licking up my neck. I shake my head, coy, fingers unzipping and pulling and *finally* stroking his perfect cock between my hands. He is huge, thick and veined.

"I need you," he whispers, forehead against mine.

"I need to come," I say, giving him a bruising kiss and rolling the condom I always keep in my bra down the length of him. I wrap my legs around his waist, and he fills me to the hilt, fucking into me so fiercely I have no choice but to hold on. This isn't *love making*.

No.

This is two humans embarking on something filthy and primal. Desperate and bone-shaking. He buries his face in my neck, cock stroking every nerve ending inside of me, thumb on my clit. I'm going to orgasm.

I'm going to orgasm with this handsome near-stranger fucking me practically through the wall. I can hear my screams of pleasure, the sounds of his groans and our bodies coming together echoing in the small room. It is so goddamn hot that I climax, shuddering in his arms with my name on his lips. He falls right after me, and we collapse against the sink.

A minute goes by, or maybe an hour. The kiss he gives me is a promise. As he slowly slides out of me, I hear something. A moan, maybe.

And then I hear it again.

Louder, this time.

Curious, I walk to the wall, pressing my ear against it. And hear, distinctly, the sounds of fucking.

Grant wraps himself around me, breath stirring the hair on my neck. "You're an inspiration, darlin'," he says, laughing softly. He is already hardening against me, hands skimming the hem of my dress. Lifting. Revealing.

"As soon as you can..." I sigh, feeling him drop to his knees, tongue licking up my thighs. "You're going to fuck me.

Again." He groans his answer as I listen through the wall—moans turning to grunts, a steady, rhythmic pounding.

I close my eyes, a million fantasies springing to life.

And then I get what I deserve.

~

I WAS STANDING in the pantry with my ear pressed to the wall. Chef had just fired three of my tables, and I was holding a heavy tray filled with crème brûlée for the snooty assholes at table six.

My feet ache. My back is killing me. I'm scheduled to be on the clock for another four hours.

And all I want in this whole damn world is to keep listening to the hot couple fuck in the bathroom.

I'd just slipped in for a second, to grab an extra salt shaker, when I heard her moaning. They'd been all over each other all night. Her: curvy with wild curls. Him: tall, dark, and too handsome. They were the kind of people whose sex noises you *wanted* to hear.

And now, with my entire body pressed to the wall, her deep, throaty moans and his heavy breathing have me almost panting. I can practically *hear* how hard he's fucking her. And I haven't had sex in so long—good sex, that is. I was staring down a nine-month dry spell, and my vibrator just wasn't cutting it anymore.

Before I'm aware—before I can even stop it—I find myself grinding against my palm, tray of food forgotten on the floor.

And that's when Declan walks in.

"What are you doing?" he asks, and immediately I roll my eyes, hoping the dim lighting will hide my blushing. I open my mouth to say something snarky, but the woman next door lets out a guttural scream so loud it's obvious what they're doing.

"Ah..." he says, coming closer to me as I spin around, facing him. "You're a pervert."

His grin is smug and heated, and I want to smash a crème brûlée into it.

"Shut the fuck up," I hiss, surprised at how breathless I sound. Declan's only been working here for three weeks, but I hated him immediately. Brash, arrogant, and a total flirt—he rakes in tips I can't *believe*—winking at me every night before he saunters home, broad shoulders stretching his uniform.

He's sexy, too sexy, with a deep, scratchy voice and a smile that makes me weak in the knees.

I hate that.

"Hmmm," he says, taking three more steps until he's right in front of me, pushing my back against the wall. Up close, I can't stop staring into his eyes.

One hand reaches forward, cupping my cheek.

"You like to listen. I like that," he says, thumb caressing. I shake my head.

"You have no idea what you're talking about," I say, but his mouth is suddenly on me, and he's kissing me like I've never been kissed before. *Gone with the Wind*-style, passionate and *searing*. On pure instinct, I yank him closer. Wrap my legs around his waist and let him lift me up against the wall.

Declan pulls back. "I've wanted to do that since the first moment I met you," he says, running his tongue up the column of my throat. I'm mindless with a lust so swift I can't remember how I got here, only that I don't want to ever leave.

"Really? You want me?" I groan, as he nibbles on my ear, one hand roughly squeezing my breast. The sexiest guy I've *ever* met? The waiter that has women and men half-fainting in adoration every night?

"Fuck yes, love. I think about you every goddamn second of the day. Have wanted to take you in this pantry so many times."

He kisses me again, so hard my lip starts to bleed. Between my legs, he is dry-fucking me with such intensity I orgasm, bright as a lightning bolt.

Declan slaps a hand over my mouth to keep me quiet, and that just turns me on more. It was filthy and illicit. Two coworkers meeting in a small, dark room to fuck each other's brains out.

But quietly so we don't get fired.

Declan doesn't even let the sensations ebb before I feel my panties shoved to the side and his condom-covered cock pushing between the lips of my pussy.

"You are so beautiful," he rasps against my ear. "And you come like a fucking *angel*." I smile, just as the woman on the other side of the wall lets out a scream of pleasure, and it is so sexy I moan: "Fuck me *please*."

And then all I can say is a steady stream of *yes yes fuck yes* because he fucks me like a dream. Like a man straight from the fantasies I've been having for months. Thorough and deep, his strong arms pinning me in place.

His lips wreak havoc on my breasts, my nipples, my neck. He is all over me like a starving man.

"I need this," he groans, pelvis hitting my clit. "I need... fuck, every time you smiled at me. Every time you looked my way. Your ass in that skirt. Your laugh..." Declan had *pined* for me. Was pining for me. I kiss him, feeling everything tighten in my belly, another orgasm threatening to sweep me away. "I'm going to..." I pant, and against the wall, the couple has started up again, her moans right in my ear. "I'm going to... *God,* I'm going to..."

Declan's hand slaps against my mouth. "That's right, angel.

Come for me. I want you boneless and dripping. I want this sweet pussy to milk me *dry*."

I scream against his palm as stars explode across my vision, and Declan fucks himself to orgasm so skillfully I come again.

Magnificently.

My body feels like a garden with every bud bursting open to blossom.

And as we both collapse to the ground, crème brûlée everywhere, salt shakers rolling, Declan looks me in the eye.

"Go on a date with me. Please," he asks, kissing my cheek.

And I say *yes*.

WILD HORSE

*I*t's the night before everything changed.

Although I didn't know that at the time.

We're all at a night-before-the-rodeo party, the coiled tension making everyone drink a little more, laugh a little more, dance a little more.

The recklessness isn't lost on me.

The Rodeo travel schedule has been hellish, and I've spent too many sleepless nights tossing and turning, body hot from thoughts about Sam. Not that I could ever tell anyone that—I wouldn't *dare*.

But now my head is spinning from wine, my body loosening with laughter, and Sam is walking towards me with the same quiet, burning intensity I've seen when he rides. *Fearless* is what they call him – because even if he gets thrown, he'll stare down that goddamn horse until it flees for the stables.

It's not fearlessness; it's arrogance. Sam *knows* he's going to win.

So he does.

And that same arrogance is heading my way: cowboy hat, worn jeans, a white shirt buttoned up. I squirm, the wine knocking down my walled defenses. I typically avoid these things like the plague—because Sam is there, and unless I'm treating him for an injury or nodding hello at breakfast, I try my hardest to pretend he doesn't *exist*.

Yet here he is, reaching his hand forward. Lifting up his cowboy hat slightly, he pins me with a gaze that knocks the breath clear from my lungs.

"Dance with me, Doc," he says with the perfect blend of cockiness and veneration, and I hear the strains of "Tennessee Whiskey" start up, and there's a patch of dirt-floor under the twinkle lights that looks just right.

And then I'm letting myself be led, his eyes never leaving

mine, and the past feels like an old photograph, water-damaged and faded. Sam pulls me into his hard body, and I let out a long, low sigh at the contact. Which he hears, his hand tightening on the small of my back, other hand tangling in my hair. His mouth is right over my ear, and he is softly singing along.

"Just one dance," I tell him, feeling an automatic need to kick up resistance. But he shakes his head.

"You can't deny this," he says, breath feathering below my ear. "You've tried. I've watched you. You're like a wild horse that refuses to be broken."

I pull back, narrowing my eyes. His finger lifts my chin. The hand on my back moves lower, and he is this-close to cupping my ass on this dance floor.

Every cell in my body screams for him to do it.

But he stops.

"You like the chase," I say. "You like that I'm *forbidden*. The one toy you can't have." But I'm tilting my neck as his fingers dip to my collarbone. He slides his index finger down, between my breasts. Then back up, stroking. When he pulls me closer, he is huge and hard between my legs.

"And that's where you're wrong," he grins. Brazenly, his finger slips beneath my bra and strokes across my nipple. Just once, but the sensation almost sends me to my knees. Sam pulls his hand away, cupping my neck again.

Like he owns me. Like I'm *his*.

"We can talk about the past all we want, Doc. But I saw you first. You remember."

I shake my head, refusing to go down that rabbit hole.

"Look at me," he says, an edge of command in his voice. And I do because the last months with him have been emotional torture.

"You're not the forbidden fruit because that would mean

I'd once entertained the notion that you weren't mine. What you had before—" he shakes his head, still angry. "Fucking child's play."

Sam isn't wrong. My engagement had been cold, the sex bad. Sam has the swagger of a man who would give me everything I ever wanted—as many times as I demanded it.

"That doesn't make this right," I try to say, but it comes out soft.

His mouth is at my ear again. And I close my eyes, leaning against his chest, breathing in his scent.

Loving it.

Loving *him*.

"If it's not blatantly obvious, Doc, I'm in goddamn love with you. Have been since the first moment I saw you. And you can pretend you don't love me all you want..."

He pulls back, staring down at me. I want him to kiss me. I want him to lay me down on this dirt floor and take what's *his*.

I want to run away to some Vegas chapel with him.

"I'll make you mine," he promises. "Just you wait and see."

The next night, Sam takes a bad fall at the rodeo.

It was a bad ride all around, and he'd limped off the rodeo stage, waving away onlookers trying to help. I'd been the medic for this gaggle of rowdy cowboys for six months now, and if Sam was limping, he was fucking *hurt*.

He wasn't the kind of person who limped.

I find him undressing in the back stable. A twitch and his shirt slides off, the intense muscles of his back and shoulders rippling. I lick my lips, and don't even have time to admonish myself because he is turning, groaning, exposing the rigid muscles of his stomach.

Sam is scarred and dirty and sweating and beautiful.

"I see you watching, Doc," Sam says, the twang of his accent causing me to squirm.

"You fell hard," I say, remembering the way the stallion had thrown Sam against the wall, crushing him.

He winces but shakes it off.

"Ain't nothin' I haven't felt before," he says, trapping me with a steely gaze. "Pain. Even a little heartbreak. All in a day's work."

I clear my throat. "Not sure that's necessary to bring up right now," I manage as he ambles closer, dragging the cloth over his chest. Down his stomach. His jeans are worn and soft, his limp prominent. "And I need to look at that."

"I don't need you to do shit, Doc," he says. He finally reaches where I'm standing, and I have to crane my neck to make eye contact. I think he might touch me, kiss me... but he just slides past.

Sam smells like a field at sunset.

Flirting with him last night was a mistake. Too much *history*. How on earth was I going to endure another six months of these confined spaces with a man who made me feel so much?

"You're angry about last night," I say, watching him roll those soft jeans down his legs. His thick, muscled thighs flex—the thighs of a cowboy. He's not ashamed of his body, undressing like we're lovers.

"I'm not angry about last night," he says, quiet as a gathering storm.

Dangerous.

"I'm angry that I told you how I felt months ago and you've done nothing but ignore me." Sam turns back to me, cowboy hat still on, nothing but black boxer briefs hugging his trim waist. I work to keep my eyes from devouring his body.

I was hungry. So fucking *hungry*.

"You know why—" I start to say, but he's suddenly on me, backing me against the hard stable wall. He doesn't lay a hand on me, just stands, mouth a centimeter from mine.

"Tell me again, Doc."

I tilt my chin, refusing to fall. "I'm sorry about last night," I say, even though I'm not. "I'm sorry I led you on. I take full responsibility—" but Sam is kissing me, taking my lips the way he rides, fierce and possessive.

I don't stand a chance.

When he finally breaks away, the words keep tumbling. "It's because I was engaged to your brother, you big sexy *jerk*," I hiss, but he's kissing up and down my throat, and the world tilts on its axis.

"Yeah? And he fucking *left*," Sam says, tip of his tongue tracing the shell of my ear. "And I'm in love with you, Doc."

I'm definitely falling now.

"So what are you going to do about it?"

And after a life of thinking too damn much, after a life lived for others (the job my parents wanted me to have, the fiancé that was supposed to be safe), after years of timid decisions and over-thinking... I stop.

Stop thinking. Start *feeling*.

And what I'm feeling is my willful heart, pounding in my chest. I'm feeling a future with Sam, opening wide before me, bright and lovely. I feel like I want to kiss him.

So I do.

I grab his handsome face in my hands and kiss him as if the world's about to end any minute.

Sam wastes no time, swiftly picking me up and laying me down on the first hay bale he can find. He is on me, his big body a delicious weight, his hands like magic, his mouth on my breasts, my nipples, my throat.

"I love you," he keeps saying, over and over, and I finally say it back. Flip him over. Run my tongue down every single ridge of his stomach. He was so hard there, harder than anything I've ever felt.

Until my fingers land on his cock and my breath halts.

"That's years of wanting you, Doc," Sam groans, thrusting up into my fingers. His cock is velvet in my hands, and as I slowly guide the head to the back of my throat, he tears the hay in half. Grips the back of my neck, lost in sensation. I hum, spurring him on, and the words tumbling from his sweet lips are utter nonsense.

Beautiful.

His fingers slide between my legs, and I am wet for him. In an instant, he is finger-fucking me into oblivion. I'm riding his hand, sucking his cock, and the only sounds in the barn are my desperate moans. His fervent *growls*.

I am going to come like this, I can feel it, but instead he yanks my head up. Swipes a thumb over my lower lip.

"You are the most perfect thing I've ever seen on this earth," he says. "And I've thought about fucking you every second of every day."

Sam makes good on his word. Laying me down. Ripping my underwear off with his teeth. Swirling his tongue around my clit until I'm nothing but a panting, sweating bundle of nerves.

He only breaks momentarily to grab a condom, holding my gaze as he rolls it all the way down his length.

And then, only then, does he slide every inch inside me. All the way to the hilt, hitting that spot he'd been working earlier. He fucks like he kisses, and he kisses like he rides: fiercely. His fingers brand my thighs, holding them open. I try to look away but he cups my face, making me take every second of his intense gaze. A gaze that says: *you, only you.*

Sam fucks me so slowly, so deeply, so goddamn thoroughly that my orgasms come in waves, over and over, interconnected. And he is watching me come undone, sweat rolling down his chest, muscles of his stomach trembling with exertion. He comes inside me with a roar, and I kiss him, every cell in my body alive with joy.

After, as we're lying together in a heap, I think about that wedding chapel down the street. So close—my future something I can reach out and *take*. Because Sam is what I deserve.

I take a piece of hay, tying it in a ring around his left finger.

"I've got an idea," I say as his eyebrows lift in delight.

"And what would that be, Doc?" he asks, taking a similar piece of hay and starting to tie it around my finger. A smile. A promise.

Our destiny, fulfilled.

"There's this chapel down the road..."

THE HERO AND THE ROOKIE

1

NAOMI

My muscular, fire-fighting boyfriend has his head between my thighs while I try my hardest to keep quiet.

I'd snuck over to Daniel's station tonight, driven by a state of pure, carnal yearning. There'd been a spate of fires across the city, and he hadn't been properly home in a week. So I'd pulled on my sexiest lingerie and slipped into his bunk.

He'd responded by flipping me onto my back and swirling his tongue around my clit like my pussy was his favorite ice cream.

But *quiet* was the name of the game since we were also surrounded by a dozen sleeping men in similar cots. A fact that should have made me feel secretive or worried or less enthusiastic about the amazing oral sex being performed on me.

Instead... the semi-public act is making me feel *illicit*. One hand is covering my own mouth; the other is beneath the covers, threaded in Daniel's thick hair. Holding him in place.

And all around me: *men*.

Not just any men. Firefighters. And yeah, I'd tell anyone

that'd listen it didn't matter that my boyfriend was a firefighter. I didn't have a "thing" for it.

But that was a goddamn lie.

Of *course* I have a "thing" for firefighters.

And now my talented, eager boyfriend is about to bring me to climax in a room filled with them.

He stops, like the tease he is, sliding his big, hard body up my back. Turning me to my side, hitching my leg up and over his hip. Exposing me. His lips close over my neck as his thick, veined cock glides through my folds. One thrust, and he's fully seated.

We're both breathing hard through our noses, trying to stay quiet. His soft groans against my ear send goosebumps zipping up my spine. My nipples are twisted and pinched by his fingers. And my clit massaged in slow, sweet circles.

And in the bed directly across from the two of us, I can just make out the shape of the rookie.

The new recruit I'd met at a firefighter's dinner a month ago. The one with the sinful smile and handsome face. I am truly, madly, deeply in love with Daniel—but the new recruit's eyes had lingered on my body all through dinner, and I'd soaked it in.

Now, as I'm being thoroughly fucked, the rookie is jerking off. I'm sure of it. Can see his hand working beneath the covers.

Maybe even hear his short, lust-filled pants.

And it makes me *wild*. The covers drop away, and the rookie's glorious body is on display, all rippling muscle as his forearm flexes with motion, the head of his cock squeezed between strong fingers. I blink, and the rookie's head turns my way... just a little. *Almost* making eye contact.

A moan slips past my lips, and Daniel chuckles, laying three fingers over my mouth. But the rookie heard it too, head turning fully now, fist jerking. Daniel is fucking me as quietly as he can, but surely every firefighter in this room can hear the bed springs. Surely every single one of them can hear me getting fucked six ways from Sunday. And it is that fantasy that sends me rocketing over the precipice. I come with tears in my eyes, watching in amazement as the rookie comes too—head thrown back, mouth open on a silent groan.

Daniel flips me onto my stomach, presses my head against the mattress, and fucks himself to climax. I come again, still sensitive and unbelievably aroused. I bite the pillow as pleasure ripples through me, loving my sexy boyfriend.

Thinking about the rookie.

Later, as we spoon in the tiny bunk, panting and breathless, Daniel smooths the hair from my face. Kisses my cheek tenderly.

And says: "Maybe next time he can join us?"

I'm walking quickly down the winding halls of the fire station, having just brought Daniel dinner before a twelve-hour shift. We haven't spoken fully about the other night yet—about the rookie. About the hot, electric thrill I'd gotten knowing he was touching himself as he watched the two of us fuck each other like animals.

Or what Daniel had said, at the end.

Maybe next time he can join us.

No.

Daniel and I have a hot and wild sex life, but we'd never spoken before about bringing in... a third person. A man. Did he mean what he said? Was he simply caught up in the moment? Fantasies didn't always make for good realities. And I'm so lost in thought, turning and turning down the long halls, that I walk smack into the naked, hard chest of the rookie.

It startles me, and as I yelp, he reaches out, steadying me by the shoulders.

"Are you okay?" he asks with a voice like soft thunder.

Two things. The rookie is naked from the waist up, wrapped in a towel. And wet from the shower.

Okay, three things: I've never seen abs before that also had their own abs.

"Yes," I say, all the breath leaving my body at once. "I'm... sorry. I was just..." But the rookie is chuckling with a sweet smile, and I grin back. "You're clearly, well, naked, so I should..."

"I'm Carter, by the way," he says, sliding his palm against mine. Squeezing.

"Naomi," I say, entranced by the feel of his fingers.

Carter looks down, unashamed at his half-nakedness. Shrugs his broad shoulders. "You get used to walking around like this in the station. Plus, you've seen... a lot here."

I have.

I saw this gorgeous hunk of a man come all over his stomach. Saw his back arch, his fingers flex, his mouth open on a silent moan. Just as he saw me climax with Daniel's thick cock balls-deep inside of me.

The walls of the hallway are subtly pressing in, forcing us closer.

"I have seen a lot," I finally say. Carter reaches his hand toward me, almost to touch, but then drops it.

"Did you see me?" he asks hoarsely. I nod. His dark eyes are like two burning suns, setting my body alight. He takes a step closer, our bodies only a sweet, beautiful inch apart. "I saw you too."

A million responses flit through my head, and if Daniel

wasn't serious about pursuing this, then things could get really, really awkward. Fast.

Or I could experience the ultimate sexual fantasy just as fast. Carter's hard length is pressing against the towel, tempting me.

I go with the second option.

"Did you like watching me?" I finally whisper, tilting my head up at him. A rumble echoes in his chest.

"More than anything," he whispers back. "He fucks you good, doesn't he?"

"Very good," I say. "And he doesn't usually share."

Carter licks his lips then glides his palm behind my neck, holding me still. Lowers his lips as if to kiss me.

"Maybe I could change his mind. What do you think?" he says against my mouth.

"I thought..." I start to stumble, "I thought you just liked me?"

Is that jealousy in my voice? Or arousal?

"That's where you're wrong," Carter says, sliding away fully. Then shifting past me in the hallway. He turns his head, tosses me a wink. "I like you both."

I'D BEEN TEASING Daniel's cock for whole minutes now—with no end in sight.

"Watch," I command as my fingers glide up and down the thick crown of Daniel's perfect, heavy dick. The two of us are staring into the mirror, his back pressed to my breasts, and my fingers are moving slow as molasses.

Daniel is a wild, coiled, panting mess—on edge and yearning for release.

But I have a question for him.

"Sweetheart," I purr with another delicious drag of my fingers. The way his abs flex should be outlawed in this country. "Do you remember the other night? In the cot?"

The two of us, fucking in a room full of men. The rookie, jerking off to the sight of my climax.

Daniel—interested.

Carter—interested in us *both*.

Daniel struggles to keep his eyes open. "Fuck, of course," he groans. "Think about it... I think about it... shit, I think about it all the time." I speed up my fingers.

"Which part, specifically?" My other hand roams his broad chest as I imagine what another set of hands would look like stroking his beautiful body. Masculine hands.

A flicker of a grin before Daniel bites out, "When he watched you."

"Ahhh," I say, eyebrow arched. "And did you mean what you said?" My hands are flying now, and Daniel is resting his palms on the wall, forehead falling forward.

"I always keep my word, Naomi," he growls on a ragged breath. "And I want to watch him work that perfect cunt of yours."

A wildfire of heat storms my senses. "I'd like that very much," I say. "He likes you."

"He likes *you*," Daniel hisses, and he is going to come any moment now.

"No," I gently correct. "Because I asked him."

"Oh God," Daniel grunts, completely on edge. "Tell me." No jealousy, no anger. He surprises me with his complete and total willingness.

"He wants to fuck you," I whisper in his ear. "And I want to watch you come with a cock inside you."

And then my hot, fire-fighting boyfriend climaxes with a roar of pleasure, shooting across the mirror, a dirty grin and

The Hero and the Rookie

Naomi on his lips. I kiss the space between his shoulder blades, desperately turned on and desperately intrigued. Daniel knew that I was bisexual, equally attracted to women as I was to men.

And he was open and kinky, and I'd always wondered... if...

Based on his reaction, I might have been right all along. But I am stunned from my thoughts as Daniel lifts me up over his shoulder and throws me backward on the bed. Dives his face between my legs with a greedy lick.

"Now tell me more..." he says.

And I do.

2

DANIEL

I'm standing beside Carter in the station bathroom, both of us shaving. Behind us are the sounds of the other firefighters, showering and laughing, and men keep walking in and out of the small space as my razor slowly glides across my skin.

Every so often, Carter locks eyes with me in the mirror, and a frisson of electricity passes between us.

He knows.

For the past week, Naomi and I have been engaging in the kinkiest fucking sex of my life, taunting and teasing each other with the fantasy of bringing another man into our bed. It had been a week of hot, erotic surprises for me. I'd always suspected I was also attracted to men but never met anyone who drew my eye.

Except for the rookie. Who is standing next to me, towel wrapped around his waist, chest bare and glistening with moisture.

The two of us are keenly aware that we have no privacy, and as desperate as I am to ask him what all of this means—if he's really serious about fucking the two of us at the same time—I can't.

Carter knocks his razor against the sink. "I saw your lovely girlfriend last week," he finally says, and my cock hardens at the scrape in his voice.

"Yeah?" I ask nonchalantly, tilting my neck and checking my handiwork. "What did you talk about?"

Carter smirks because I know what they talked about. Naomi had all-but-propositioned him in the hallway, and Carter had said he'd liked both of us.

Both.

Meaning me too. Later, as she had jerked me off in front of that mirror, it was all too easy to imagine the full, smirking lips of the rookie wrapped around my cock, sucking me off enthusiastically. My hands tangled in his hair, the grunting sounds he'd make.

I'd exploded in climax, and later, as I'd licked my girlfriend's pussy for an hour, I'd gotten off again as she described what it would be like to take us both.

Fuck us both.

There'd been no jealousy. No anger. It was surprising really—just an honest acceptance that he was going to come into our lives.

"Oh, just what she wanted me to help you guys with. This weekend. The uh..." Carter blushes a little as two other men walk by, cracking a joke my way. I laugh, but it's distracted.

"The what?" I press. Against his towel, his cock is long and hard. So is mine.

"The work you needed done. In the... bedroom," he says then softly chuckles. I bite my lip to keep from joining him.

"Right," I finally say, glancing over my shoulder. "She mentioned you were interested." A long pause. "In helping."

"Very," he says immediately. "I'm very interested." He holds my gaze for a fraught minute, and both of us are semi-panting.

"You uh... you've helped people before?" I ask, dipping my face beneath a spray of water to rinse the shaving cream. When I look up, his fingers are on his cock, pressing against the fabric. I groan audibly—can't help it—and end up coughing into my hand to cover it up.

"Not a lot. But a few times. It takes a really special—"

Another group of guys walk by, slapping me on the back.

"—it takes a really special friendship," he finishes. "I don't just help anyone."

I nod as if we're discussing the remodeling I need help with in my bedroom. Which we're not.

We're talking about the two of us fucking the hell out of my gorgeous girlfriend.

Maybe we're even talking about fucking each *other*.

And *Christ,* could I get any harder?

"We should talk," I say, eyes on his blue ones. "About this weekend. You and I. Get some... details straight."

A charming smile. Fuck, he's handsome. "I'd like that," he says softly.

I go to turn because it is too tight and too small and too hot in this room. And as I leave, the rookie hooks his hand around my arm and shoves me backward against the wall. Cups my face and gives me an urgent kiss. My first kiss with a man; the first time I feel a man's lips on mine, firm and insistent. The rough scrape of his remaining stubble, his chest brushing against mine and the sense of coiled, hungry energy thrumming beneath his muscles.

I kiss him back, although that doesn't really paint an accurate picture of the way my tongue dives against his. The way I thread my fingers into his hair and yank.

Then the moment is over, all too soon, because another

group of people is coming, and Carter lets me go. Swipes his thumb across his lips and gives me a searing look.

"What happens next?" I whisper, straightening my towel with trembling hands.

"That's up to you," he says, before sauntering out of the room.

3

NAOMI

I am basking in the glow of having two deliciously handsome firefighters look at me like they plan on fucking me into next week.

Which they do.

The rookie is here. In the cozy apartment I share with Daniel. He'd arrived not two hours earlier to have a pre-threesome dinner I assumed would be awkward. But we'd split a bottle of expensive red wine, and Carter had laughed and flirted and charmed both of us. And now we'd drunk enough wine and were relaxing by the fire, and I sincerely hope Carter knows what happens next. He gives me a hungry, fevered look as Daniel strokes his fingers at the nape of my neck.

I want the rookie.

I want my boyfriend.

I want them both at the same time.

"Are you nervous?" Carter asks, taking one final sip of wine. Like a leopard, he stands and stalks to the couch where we are curled next to each other. Kneels in front of me. But doesn't touch.

"Yes," I say, honesty spurred on by his sexy nearness. The rookie looks at Daniel.

"Yes," he grunts, clearing his throat. All three of us laugh a little breathlessly as the fire dances a few feet away.

"You've... done this before?" I ask, and he nods, biting his lip thoughtfully.

"You're a beautiful couple," he says, looking to Daniel. Some kind of permission must have been given because his hand lands on the side of my face, thumb sweeping against my lips. "I thought about the two of you a lot, even before you fucked in front of me."

I bite my lip, fighting a blush. "We thought you were asleep."

"Bullshit," Carter teases softly, and the blush races up my throat. "You liked it, beautiful girl."

"She did," Daniel says behind me. "I did too." The tension between the three of us is like pulsing, electric lightning, waiting to strike.

"We can just do that if you want. I'll fuck my fist while you fuck each other." The rookie gives me a kind smile, and then I'm startled by the gruffness of my boyfriend.

"No," he says, leaning forward. Wrapping his fingers around the rookie's neck. "That's not what's happening tonight."

I am breathless, in a trance.

"And what's that, handsome?" Carter asks as Daniel lowers his lips and gives him a fervent kiss. Almost angry. The sight of my gorgeous boyfriend kissing this equally gorgeous man sends me up in flames. I try to sneak my fingers beneath my dress, but Carter grabs my wrist, eyes still closed, lips still devouring.

When Daniel finally releases him, they both give me a chiding look.

"You're going to come on his cock," Daniel says, giving me the same hungry kiss. "In fact, he's going to give you as many orgasms as I demand. Isn't that right?"

Carter is in on it now, slowly unbuttoning his shirt, revealing the ridged muscles of his upper body. "That's fucking right."

"And then... and then what?" I pant because Daniel is pinching my nipples as I watch this sexy strip-tease. Carter frees his cock, and I almost pass out at the sight of it.

"Then he's going to come with my cock inside of him," Daniel whispers against my ear, and all I can do is whimper. Carter slides the straps down on my dress, working the zipper, and suddenly it is pooled on the floor.

I'd worn lingerie for the occasion—stockings and a garter. Both men hiss with pleasure, and it gives me the sweetest, headiest feel of *power*. Both men lean forward, taking a nipple between their lips.

I don't recognize the sound I make. It's not even *human*.

"Then what?" I whimper, spreading my legs, already needing more.

"And then?" Daniel says, groaning as the rookie palms his cock. "Then you take us both."

4

DANIEL

I'm not sure who I want to kiss more: my girlfriend or the rookie.

So far, I've watched him strip from his clothes, baring a body that had me erect in seconds. I'd groaned as he'd wrapped his strong fingers around my cock—the grip so unlike that of a woman's.

Not better, just different.

And now I was watching my gorgeous girl, decked out in lingerie like a goddamn pin-up model, and she has her legs wrapped around Carter on the floor.

"Remember," I whisper as his palms glide around to her ass, pulling her close so she can grind against him. "As many orgasms as I say."

I thread my fingers in her long hair and twist and yank her throat back. She hisses and moans as I hover my lips over her ear. "Her tight little cunt likes to play."

Carter arches an eyebrow, fingers gliding between her legs, and I know when he's found her clit because she bites her lip.

It's hot, hotter than I ever *imagined*, to watch her be touched by another man. Pleased by another man. She's grinding against his palm as I lower my lips to her neck and he sucks her nipples into his mouth.

My eyes lock with Carter's, an erotic spark dancing between us. He languorously licks her, lips teasing, and I mimic his motions on her neck.

I want to kiss him.

I want to kiss *her*.

I want our bodies to clash together, fucking and getting fucked until we come so many times we can't stand up.

Carter's fingers shift, finger-fucking her with such precision she climaxes a minute later, gasping and screaming, trapped between two hard, male bodies.

"So pretty," he says, kissing her gently, caressing her hair. She has collapsed against his chest, half-laughing, half-panting, and suddenly I feel Carter's fingers on my cock again. Stroking expertly.

"I can make you feel good too," he promises, squeezing my balls roughly. I almost choke, the sensation raw and real, and then I'm kissing him hungrily. Naomi sighs, wiggling in pleasure, lips dancing along my jaw as Carter thrusts his tongue between my lips.

I bite it, tug on his lower lip with my teeth, and his fingers falter.

The rookie likes a little pain.

"Fuck her," I command. "Give her this cock." The words are barely out of my mouth before Naomi shoves Carter to the ground and takes every inch of him. He groans, fingers tight on her hips, and I kiss her as she rocks back and forth. She strokes my cock as she takes the rookie's, and I never want this experience to end.

"I need to taste you," I rasp. "Need to taste you while you take him." And then I'm on my hands and knees next to Carter's tight, muscular body. I lick a path down his abdomen,

The Hero and the Rookie

and he shudders. I swallow hard at the sight in front of me: wide cock stretching my girlfriend's pussy. I've never done this before, and I'm nervous and unsure, but my tongue darts out, licking him at his base, and Carter lets out a string of curses.

"Fuck that's hot," Naomi groans, holding my head in place as I lick and lick. Carter is desperate and grunting, and though I hate to leave, my girlfriend's clit is begging for attention. I suck the small bud into my mouth, head moving with her motions, and she wails.

I can't get enough, tongue dancing between her clit and his sliding cock. I am driving them wild.

They are driving *me* wild.

And that's when I feel a finger, sliding down my ass.

All three of us still at once, my muscle tight with apprehension. Part of me knew this might happen tonight, and I'd thought about it.

Fuck I'd thought about it.

"I want to make you feel good here," Carter groaned, pressing just a little at the tight ring of muscle I'd never explored. "But only if it's okay."

I look up at Naomi, who is flushed and aroused and so beautiful I feel my heart break. She strokes my face and I lean up to kiss her—starved for her lips. Eyes on hers, I whisper, "Do it."

I bury my face back into my girlfriend's cunt, curl my tongue against her clit, and hiss through the bite of pain as Carter's finger probes. Pain then overwhelming, shocking, knee-trembling pleasure emanates from where his finger strokes.

"What the fuck," I groan, laying my head on his stomach, too overwhelmed. Naomi strokes my hair as Carter strokes inside me, and the world is bright with ecstasy.

"Jesus, I can't..."

I take my cock in my hands and groan, Carter's fingers moving, my tongue back to its decadent dance between his cock and her clit. All three of us, surging toward release, the sounds of our bodies coming together pushing me to a sharp climax.

I come on Carter's stomach, jets of it on his abs. Naomi shudders with her own orgasm as Carter's back arches off the ground. Both of us watch his handsome face contort with pleasure, the utter sexiness of it, the flush of his chest and the smirk that tugs at his lips.

Naomi collapses onto his chest as I fall to my back, stroking her hair, eyes locked with Carter's.

"Did it feel good?" he asks, fingers smoothing down my side.

"Goddammit yes," I say, leaning in to claim his mouth. "I haven't... that was my first time doing... that."

He groans softly against my lips, and I can already feel my hunger growing again.

"I'm glad I could be the one," he says, squeezing Naomi tight against his chest. "Now what should we do next?"

5

NAOMI

I'm not sure what to do with the fantasy coming true right before my eyes.

I've thought about it.

Oh, I've thought about it. Who wouldn't? I have a giant, strapping, fire-fighting boyfriend, and at night, when I touch myself, it's not another woman that I fantasize him being with.

It's another man.

Like exactly what's happening in front of me now. I am laying on the floor, sated from my half-dozen orgasms, and Carter is showing Daniel just how he likes to be touched.

Carter's head is tilted back in euphoria as Daniel's lips trail down his abs and lick along his hip bones. Tentative. A little unsure. But when he reaches Carter's thick cock, he growls low in his throat.

"Wrap your lips around it," Carter groans, and Daniel arches an eyebrow at the soft command. But he's too aroused —I can see that—so he does as he's told.

And I watch my boyfriend suck cock for the first time.

I commit this moment to memory: Carter, arching off the floor. Daniel, taking this man's cock to the very back of his throat. He loves it—I can see that he loves it—and I desperately want to get off, but I'm saving myself.

For when they both take me.

So instead I let the pleasure build inside of me, unfurling gently beneath my skin. And then our rookie is gasping and shuddering and begging for my boyfriend to fuck him. Daniel takes the lube, still a little unsure, and spreads it down the length of his cock.

"And then..." he asks the rookie, clearing his throat. Carter takes Daniel's wet fingers and slides them between his ass. I watch his wrist flex, and then both men groan out loud.

"Goddammit you're tight," Daniel says, biting his lip, and then he leans down and gives Carter a rough kiss. I want to be between the two of them so badly my pussy aches, but I wait.

It will be worth it.

"This feels okay?" Daniel gasps, kissing Carter and working his fingers. Carter can barely speak, just nods his head. Kisses my boyfriend with sweet passion as he rolls a condom down his dick.

"Need more," he finally bites out. "Need you." Like clockwork, Daniel's eyes flick up to mine, seeking permission. And I nod enthusiastically.

I watch my sexy, strapping boyfriend slide his cock into another man's ass.

And my life is complete. Because I'm discovering there is no greater turn-on for me than watching him get turned on by someone else. Get pleasure from someone else. I experience an illicit thrill, a fervent euphoria. I'm not even touching myself, but as Daniel's hips thrust forward, my back arches off the couch.

Both men groan raggedly, Carter wrapping his legs around Daniel's waist, bringing him down for a kiss.

Another thrust, and I swear to God Daniel's inside of me.

My fingers itch to touch my clit, but I hold off again. I bite my lip at the same time Carter bites my boyfriend.

Which causes him to hiss with pain, yanking Carter's hair in response.

"Your cock is amazing," Carter moans, fingers scratching into the other man's back. "Fuck, it's so…" but his words are cut off when Daniel wraps his fingers around his cock and tugs. I arch off the couch again as he pants and moans, as Daniel begins fucking this man with wild abandon. No more tentative movements—now he moves with a confidence, a deep knowing.

And it is so fucking *sexy*.

With a shudder and a curse, Daniel pulls out, flips Carter over, and takes him from behind. And I crawl over, loving the smirk on Daniel's face as he watches my naked body. Loving the feel of Carter's lips on mine, his desperate moans. Daniel sits back on his heels, bringing Carter onto his lap, and works him fast, yanking him down onto his cock. Carter's head falls back onto Daniel's shoulder, and before I can stop myself, I am gliding my lips down the length of his cock.

Daniel thrusts, and my lips suck, and Carter is shooting his come down my greedy throat. His hands tighten in my hair, holding me there, and when he finally lets go, Daniel puts him on his knees and fucks into him like an animal. My boyfriend grunts his release, muscles rippling, sweat sliding down his chest.

And then it's only a moment of rest before both men pin me with a hungry look.

Because it's my turn now.

6

CARTER

I think I might be falling in love with Daniel and Naomi.

It's true that they're not the first couple I've ever played with; I've fucked my fair-share of curious couples. But I'd been drawn to Daniel from the first moment I showed up at that fire station; and the night I watched them fuck each other was easily one of the most erotic nights of my life.

Until now.

The thing is, they're so affectionate with each other. Trusting and supportive. Fuck, this is the first time they've ever *done* this, and within minutes, my fingers were buried in her pretty cunt as he stroked my cock.

They were eager for it, hungry, and instead of jealousy, there was only this beautiful exploration of each other's bodies.

"We're going to get you ready now sweetheart," I growl into Naomi's ear, laying her on her side. I lock eyes with Daniel, who nods his approval. "If you're going to take both of us," I say, gliding my fingers down to the tight muscle of her ass, "I want you begging for it by the time we're done with you. Understand?"

I kiss sweetly along the back of her neck as Daniel kisses her deeply. And then he kisses me, groaning against my lips. He'd just fucked the hell out of me not twenty minutes ago, but we're both rock-hard again.

Daniel slides down Naomi's body, pulling her leg over his shoulder. Immediately, she moans, his tongue darting against her clit. He looks up at me, and I smile. As he eats her pussy, I keep pressing my body against hers, sliding my finger into her ass. She gasps, shudders, squeezes her eyes tightly. And then... a total euphoria comes over her. Daniel sucks her clit, and I open and spread her. Prepping her to take my cock.

"Relax, beautiful girl," I whisper, dipping my head to lap at her nipples. She makes an inhuman sound of approval, and I slide another finger inside of her. I glance down her body, seeing his fingers working between the folds of her cunt, tongue swirling against her clit. She's filled with my fingers now. Completely.

"Does this feel good?" I whisper, and she can barely answer. Her body is already shaking. So I press a kiss at the base of her spine. Then lower. And lower, sliding my tongue down her back, her hips, the curve of her ass.

Then my tongue joins my fingers, dipping into that tight ring, and she absolutely *wails*. I tangle my legs with Daniel, and his big hand comes around to grip my neck. He is growling against her skin, and I'm grinding my cock against his stomach, and Naomi is shrieking and coming between the two of us.

She tries to shove both of us away, but we refuse to move, and the two of us work our fingers and our tongues until she's cresting again.

"What the ever-loving fucking *fuck* was that," she pants, flopping onto the floor, and the two of us laugh against her skin. He is hard.

I am *so* hard.

And she's ready.

7

NAOMI

I was more than ready to take two cocks.

My body is boneless and begging. I've come so many times I've lost count, but the two muscled, sexy men pressed against me are making damn sure I can take one more.

"You're trembling," Daniel says against my lips, smoothing his palm over my hair. Caressing the back of my neck. Carter is at my back, massaging my hips, my thighs.

"Just excitement," I say, kissing him passionately. "I want you both. Want you both so badly."

Behind me, I feel the rookie chuckle softly, licking up my spine.

"Greedy girl," he murmurs, and I can only nod. Because he's right.

Daniel has some kind of wordless communication with Carter, and then he is hooking my leg over his hip, gliding his cock inside of me.

"Oh God," I moan, his fingers bruising my waist, lips crushing the pulse at my throat. "Still feels so amazing."

And it does. I was worried I'd be sore or tender, overly

stimulated. But instead it's like an orgasm that hasn't fully ended, a lingering shock of pleasure that pulses through my body. Daniel groans in delight, and for a few minutes, it's just the two of us, rocking against each other. Eyes locked in passion.

"Are you sure?" he asks. "I want you to be sure, baby."

Behind me, Carter hovers his lips over my ear. Waiting.

"Fuck yes," I pant. There's a shift of movement behind me, lube dripping down my ass.

"We're going to make you feel so good," Carter promises, holding me still for a moment. I moan in frustration, needing friction, movement, slick thrusting. Daniel plays with my nipples, fingers my clit, sucks my tongue into his mouth. A distraction.

The rookie nudges his cock into my ass. Just an inch. I squeal, although it's not entirely in pain.

"It's okay, sweetheart," Carter soothes, caressing my hair. His fingers dance along my breasts, holding one up for Daniel to lick. I make a strangled sound, and the rookie slides in another inch.

"Oh Christ," I pant, holding stock still. I want more I want more I want—

"More, fuck, more," I whimper as both men kiss me. Kiss each other. Another inch, and Daniel rocks into me at the same time. Light and sound explode inside my body. Both firefighters are grunting with effort, sweat gliding down their chests. Hands everywhere. Lips everywhere.

"More," I beg, one final time, and both men slide entirely inside me.

I scream for a long time as the most exquisite pleasure tears through me. As if reading each other's minds, they rock in tandem, sliding in the same slow, but steady, rhythm. Building me up for what I already know will be the most intense orgasm of my life. Daniel spreads my ass cheeks, watches the rookie's cock take me there. Carter slaps Daniel on the ass, hard, and he speeds up his movements. I am pinned between both, two sets of hands on my nipples. Then two sets of fingers on my clit.

"So fucking tight," Carter swears, biting my shoulder. Staring at Daniel. "Tell me you've taken this ass before."

Daniel shakes his head, moaning, watching me with fire in his eyes. "Not yet. But I will."

I shiver at the delicious threat because Carter's cock is hitting some beautiful angle that makes Daniel's cock slide even deeper.

"Now tell me what her pussy feels like," Carter demands, reaching forward and grabbing Daniel's chin. "Look at me and tell me."

"Fuck, so wet," he grunts, his rhythm faltering for a moment. I am hanging by a thread, watching this. "She's so perfect. Lets me get so fucking deep."

"Goddammit yes," Carter groans. "Rub that clit, handsome. Make our pretty girl come apart."

I've never seen my boyfriend follow orders so willingly, but he does, as desperate to please Carter as I am. The rookie bottoms out inside of me as my boyfriend begins driving between my legs. And when his thumb lands on my clit I go off in a shower of sparks.

I scream so loudly Carter covers my mouth, laughing huskily in my ear, stroking me as my pussy clenches and grips and climaxes for what feels like a full minute. My sexy firemen come not a moment later, and I've never heard anything hotter in my life than the sounds of two men, coming undone, muttering dirty phrases and growling against my skin.

They are beautiful in their ecstasy.

And I've never felt more beautiful. More worshipped,

more loved, more cherished. Because the three of us hold each other for a long time on that floor, sweat finally drying, breath finally slowing. When I wake the next morning, I am crushed between the two of them, hands entwined.

I slide out from between their bodies, cataloging the image of my boyfriend, naked, with another hot firefighter. The sun drifts through the windows, the spring breeze like a caress. Because it's a new day.

It was just the two of us before. Happy, in love. But now?

Now it was going to be three.

DID YOU TOUCH YOURSELF?

*O*ur hero is nothing but demands this evening.

A long dinner together—the kind with candles and expensive wine and a dish you couldn't pronounce but nevertheless devoured. Our hero had been his usual warm, funny self, winking at you over the candlelight. Holding your hand beneath the table. Looking dapper as fuck in his suit, his eyes never lingering past the pearls around your throat.

But you know what a night like tonight means to him—to the hungry beast that lives beneath his skin, barely caged. Barely restrained, even though on the drive back to your house, he is sweetly stroking your wrist, delighting you with some silly story from work. You're still laughing when you step through the door, climb the stairs up to your bedroom. Still airy and almost light-headed from the wine and the dinner and the way his dark eyes never left yours. He is like that always, willing for you to be the subject of his laser focus, his trust, his all-consuming love.

But you know what's coming, and as he leans against the counter, fiddling with his cuff-link, you sit primly on the bed.

Awaiting instruction.

Because our hero has a way with *instructions*.

He crosses his long legs in front of himself, leaning back fully. A careful arch of his brow.

"Did you touch yourself this week?" he asks.

You shake your head vigorously. It was his most important demand, and you (almost) never break it.

"No," you say, swallowing. "Sir."

He looks like he doesn't believe you.

"So that means you haven't had an orgasm in..." he consults his watch, counting back the days. "A week. Correct?"

You nod. You've been gone on business, and even though our hero sent you a string of filthy text messages—complete with descriptions—his only demand was that you don't masturbate.

You obeyed his demand, even though you ached so much you couldn't sleep, your dreams fevered with memories of your time spent together.

"Prove it," he says, sliding his hands into his pockets. He could have been talking to you about the weather. Having a meeting. Certainly not sucking all the oxygen out of the room with his domineering presence.

"How?" you ask, already spreading your legs. You weren't wearing any underwear—another demand.

"Fuck yourself," he says, tilting his head. "I'll watch. And time you," he says, tapping on his watch. "You're a greedy, dirty girl. Greedy girls can get themselves off quickly when they've waited a week or more."

The air between you stretches tight with tension.

"Isn't that right?"

You swallow roughly. "Yes," you say. "That's right." Already, you are almost dizzy with arousal, moisture seeping down your thighs. Our hero knows what this does to you, the suit and the candles and the demands. It is your entire life, the rush you crave.

He snaps his fingers.

"Dress off," he says, still leaning against the fucking counter. Fully dressed. Voice light, although you can hear the knife's edge of it.

You stand, lifting your dress up and off. Only you can see the way his jaw works, the tension in his fingers. This is torture for him, but our hero would do anything for you.

"Lay back on the bed," he says, voice strained. Your eyes flick down, and you can see the outline of his cock against his suit pants. "Spread your legs."

You're elevated on a pillow so you can watch our hero, and

when you spread your legs, he almost snaps his cufflinks off. Your heart soars—even after all this time, he is hungry for you.

"Ninety seconds," our hero says, sliding his hands back into his pockets. "That's all you get, princess." You're already nodding hungrily, sliding your fingers down to your clit.

"And if you don't come?" He says, voice silky with danger. "Then you can wait another goddamn week for that orgasm."

Ten seconds later, and you are already almost *there*. His gaze rakes up and down your prone body. You need to come, you need to come, *you need to come*, and you chant this to yourself as you circle your clit roughly, our hero watching your fingers with a look of primal hunger on his face. He is still leaning against the counter, fully dressed in his suit, but you recognize the self-control it takes for him to stay far away from you.

"God *yes*," you moan, eyes fluttering closed as your pleasure mounts.

"Eyes open," he snaps. You obey, locking on his.

"I'm sorry," you say, but it's no more than a breathless pant, and you let a fantasy play out in your mind as he glances at his watch with an arched eyebrow. You don't know how much time you have left, but you fuck yourself and remember the multiple times he's fucked you over that counter. Taken you against the wall. Eaten your pussy in the shower until you collapsed onto the tiles.

You remember the many brilliant, mind-blowing, earth-shattering orgasms he has given you, and in seconds, you are climaxing around your fingers, screaming his name, and before you can even come down, he is stalking towards the bed.

Suit on, cock out.

Flips you onto your stomach like you weigh nothing,

which is quite possible because as he grips your hips and slides his cock inside, you feel *weightless* with lust. Floating somewhere near a paradise of sensation.

Our hero is unleashed now, and there is no hope that he will be gentle. And who would want him to? You love him like this. You want him like this, his palm ringing down on your ass. His hand, tangling in your hair and shoving your face hard into the mattress. You're so aroused you just... keep coming. Over and over, clenching and moaning and screaming and sighing. He pulls out before he comes, yanking your ass up to his face so he can fuck you with his tongue, fucking your ass with his finger. Filling you everywhere.

The sounds from his mouth are rough and needy, and you are the source of this. Of all of it. Before you met, our hero fucked like a gentleman. But you've turned him into the alpha of your dreams. And the alpha of your dreams is bringing you to another orgasm with his tongue and his finger, flipping you onto your back and throwing your legs over his shoulders so he can bend you the fuck in half.

"Good girl," he says, lowering his face to yours. "Dirty girl. Greedy girl." His smile is just as dirty and just as greedy, and you grip his face in your hands as you kiss him, tasting yourself. Tasting his desire and yours, a potent mixture.

"Yours," you say, and he curses, dropping his face to your neck and pulling your skin between his teeth.

"Always yours," you chant. Our hero comes like that, explosively. Shooting you to the moon, the outer edges of our universe. A place all your own.

THE GIFT

What captivates me about my sister's fiancé is that he's a boxer in secret. He fights underground, in some dark, sunken room; fights with men stripped to the waist, fists raised and snarls on their lips. It is an image I've thought about often at night as the embers in my fireplace slowly die. I'm not sure what the feeling is. What they do to each other is pure brutality, an act almost carnal in nature, and when I think about it, I squeeze my thighs together, quelling some ache I can't diagnose.

Baron assumes no one knows, but I've seen his bloodied knuckles at dinner. Seen him wince when my sister grasps his palm as they waltz, twirling around the drawing room like clusters of birds. His eyes are shadowed with bruises, and every time our gaze meets, his burn like the embers.

What captivates me about my sister's fiancé is that he is always *watching* me. When the others have retired to play cards or badminton, the two of us sit. Not close, but close enough. The thick layers of my skirt rustle against his pant legs, and when my glove exposes the thin skin of my wrist, Baron appears... hungered.

Our conversation is always deep and intimate—he is a fan of literature, and minutes turn to hours as we discuss favorite passages and rhymes. His dark hair is curled and just slightly wild, and I want to press my gloved hands to the strands.

What captivates me about my sister's fiancé—Baron—is that he is duly betrothed to her yet has sent me a secret missive in the night. A note, written plainly, asking me to meet him here. A darkened parlour, the kind I've read about with pink cheeks, with clientele who favor the scandal pages. I've been sitting far in the corner, the darkest alcove, next to a roaring fire. My gloves have been removed, due to the heat, and my fingers flex with freedom. When he arrives, he is panting; shirt half-unbuttoned to reveal a scandalous few inches of chest. There is dark hair there, curling like the ones on his head, and I feel that ache again.

"Have you..." I ask, startled because his knuckles are blood-red. "Are you coming from there? Boxing?"

Baron grins ruefully, and my heart flutters. "I knew you'd figured it out," he says. "And yes. Yes, I have." He sits next to me—practically on top of me, or at least that's how it feels. His thigh presses against mine, hip to hip, shoulder-to-shoulder. I am frozen with desire, and his dark eyes never stray far from my lips.

"Why do you do it?" I ask. "And why did you bring me here? You know it's not... it's not right."

There's a movement beneath my skirts, a faint rustling, and at first I can't place it. I glance down, but Baron's voice intersects my thoughts. "Look at me, Alice."

And so I do, my body operating on some biological instinct. Baron is grasping my palm, bare skin to bare skin, and my body feels like a million tiny rays of light. He turns it softly, raises it to his lips. Beneath my skirts, Baron slides his strong, rough fingers around my bare knee.

I gasp—because I can't help it—and Baron's lips twitch in the firelight.

"I do it because it makes me feel alive," he rasps. "And I brought you here because I can't seem to stop thinking about you." He presses his lips to the inside of my wrist. "I brought you here because I needed somewhere private to do this." Another caress of his lips, firmer this time, and his hand is gliding beneath my petticoat. Past my garter and the tops of my stockings. I have never had a man's hand on me like this before.

Although I had... *thought* about it.

Thought about it in the same way I thought about boxing.

The Gift

"What are you going to do?" I ask, voice trembling. Baron's tongue darts out and gives a hot, wet lick along the inside of my wrist. I make a sound, something primal, and he glances behind him. The room is almost empty, and its patrons seem otherwise indisposed, but still. We are in public. With my sister's fiancé.

"Stay quiet, my darling," he says, kissing and licking my wrist as his fingers dive beneath the oceans of fabric that enclose my most secret area. "I realized something the other day, you see." Two fingers land on my sex, land on an area I'd discovered the other night. A small button that made me jump when I brushed against it.

Baron wasn't brushing against it... he was lightly, gently, circling it. Like it was a delicate bud about to blossom.

"I realized I made a terrible mistake because I've become betrothed to the wrong sister." His smile was wide and loving, and I smile broadly back. "And I have an idea, a plan, to change the course of our situation, but I wanted to give you something first. A gift. So that you could see the kind of husband I'd be for you."

Baron's eyes close as he kisses my pulse point again—kisses it deeply, tongue swirling. At the same time his fingers increase their pressure, moving beneath my bountiful skirts, and the room feels like it's tilting. Or spinning. My breath is coming faster, and I feel quite like I'm running somewhere—but unable to see the finish line.

"I don't expect much," I say, flirting, "I just expect my husband to love me as much as he loves books. And to let me dress his boxing wounds, of course." Baron chuckles against my wrist but then pins me with a greedy gaze. Holding it, his tongue roves around my wrist wetly, fingers working with speed. "So what..." I am panting now. "What gift did you have in mind?"

Baron leans forward daringly, pressing a kiss to the swell of my breasts above my corset. One, two, three kisses, and I have to swallow a high moan. The finish line, the cliff, whatever I am racing toward, seems to be... appearing. Quickly. Baron's lips trail up the swell... up the column of my throat... along my jaw. He smells musky. Bloody. Like man and sweat.

"Pleasure, darling," he says, rasping against my ear, and I... I... *climax*. Writhing like an electric wire, grasping at his shirt, wailing into his shoulder. The feeling is better than books and dancing and music and moonlight. The feeling is... indescribable. Pure ecstasy. When I finally pull back, his mouth is an inch from mine, ghosting over my lips. So handsome I could cry. "If we wed, Alice, I will give you that gift every day of your life. As often as you ask for it. I promise you that."

"Can I do that for you?" I ask, uncertain. He swallows roughly, eyes dark.

"Yes, my darling. Yes, you can. We can do it together, I promise."

THE CEREMONY in the church had been splendid; Baron truly dashing in his attire, dark eyes bright with laughter. When he'd kissed me at the appropriate time, his lips had been light and sincere. But his hand had curled around my neck, holding me in place, and something about that touch had felt thrilling and indecent. A claiming—my body yielding itself to a new master.

My sister (newly, and happily, married to Baron's friend) had spoken to me in furtive tones about tonight's "obligations." Eyes down, cheeks pink, she'd spoken of a man's desires. The fear some women felt when they first saw a man's sex organ. My sister had gripped my hand, reminding me that

The Gift

sensual pleasure was not always part of every marriage and to not view our union as anything less if that was the case.

Except I'd already been given The Gift. Just once, six months earlier, and since then, Baron and I had not strayed back to that dark, alluring club. Since then, our interactions had been free from scandal. But as my female relations scurried off, fans over their faces, I couldn't help but feel wise beyond their years.

Wise and... aching. Every time Baron caught my eye across the room, there was a *pulsing*—steady as a drumbeat—right between my legs. An awareness on my skin.

Did all newlyweds feel this way before their honeymoon night?

Or was this Baron's doing?

It was past midnight before our guests had cause to excuse themselves, and by then, every touch of Baron's seemed to accelerate that drum-beat pulse. His hand on my elbow. His palm low on my back. The feel of his gravelly voice at my ear, whispering sweet words. My new husband was watched hungrily by the women in the room, and I feel a smug satisfaction at their yearning. Tilt my chin higher, lean back into his touch.

Because Baron is mine now.

And as I stare into the fireplace, room finally silent and empty, it is Baron's solid weight against my back. His lips on my neck, trailing teasing kisses from my shoulder to my ear.

"Husband," I gasp, body arching into his. Arching and feeling for the first time, *even* through my many layers, the hard length of his... cock. A word I'd just learned and quite liked the sound of.

"Wife," he whispers, hands sliding down my arms to clasp my fingers. I arch again, and my new husband groans against my skin.

It is utterly thrilling.

"My sister told me I would be afraid of this night, but I'm finding it hard to fear something that feels so..." I trail off. Baron is sliding the fabric of my dress down the smooth curve of my shoulder. Hot mouth on my skin, the wet point of his tongue.

And then... his teeth.

"Something so what?" he asks softly.

"Delicious," I finally manage. Feeling suddenly bold, I reach my hand between our bodies, grasp a cock that feels like thick steel. My husband curses, voice ragged, and I feel *power*.

"Do you fear your husband, my darling?" he asks, rocking a bit into my hand. The two of us are warmed by flickering firelight, eyes half-open, mouths already gasping.

"No," I sigh, half-laughing. "I *want* my husband." I turn my head, and our lips meet in a passionate, searing kiss. Behind me, his fingers work the buttons of my heavy gown, and I am suddenly desperate to be rid of it. Baron's mouth stays on mine, and a minute later, my wedding dress drops to a colorful pool at my feet. I step out, gingerly aware that in the light my shift and petticoat are practically transparent.

"And I very much want my wife," Baron says, eyes roaming my body. I smile at him, and his answering grin has my heart beating at a reckless pace. He turns me again, back toward the fire, lips landing at the base of my neck. "Every inch of you pleases me," he says, silently working the stays of my shift. Exposing small gaps of my skin. "Every inch of you makes me delirious with desire."

I feel quite delirious myself with my dashing husband peeling off my clothing like skin from a fruit. Reverently, like I was a sacred object to be worshipped. I was unaware that the curve of my spine was such an erogenous area, but his lips kissing every inch are making The Gift feel close.

The Gift

Baron's large palm rests between my now-bare shoulder blades, and he pushes me forward gently. My hands land on the fireplace mantle, layers falling open. The curve and swell of my backside is now exposed, and when his mouth lands there, it grows hungry and greedy.

"Look at this," he says, stroking the round globes, caressing, mouth tasting. "Look at how gorgeous you are here."

I realize that I've been making a keening sound, eyes shut. Baron spreads the globes apart, and the feeling is truly indecent. Indecent and electrifying.

My sex keeps clenching, and I'm not sure why that is. And as Baron licks his way closer, he starts to chuckle.

"Something funny, husband?" I ask, although it's more of a pant. His fingers stroke along my inner thighs, which are wet with God-knows-what.

"This wetness," he rasps, "is your body telling me you are aroused." His tongue flattens, laps it up, and I shiver. "You taste like peaches on a summer day. So ripe." Fingers wrap around my thighs, holding me in place, and then Baron's tongue touches me *there*. Inside.

Inside.

I cry out at the shock of it, the ecstasy, his tongue moving in some ancient rhythm set by the gods of pleasure—because how else would my husband know what to do? Both of us—husband and wife—are groaning, and when his tongue slows down, I press back shamelessly, seeking *more*.

"Baron please," I beg, but I'm not sure what I'm begging for. But then his gentle thumb lands on my greedy button—the spot where The Gift springs from—and pleasure surges forth like water from a fountain. I cry out again, bucking against his mouth, and then I am cresting like that day in the parlor. Cresting and racing and reaching and—

Ecstasy.

I don't even have time to really descend from the mountain before Baron—my husband—is lifting me in his strong arms and carrying me to the marriage bed. His handsome face holds a slight smirk, and when I pull him in for a kiss, he tastes like... like the earth. And a bit like peaches.

"What was that?" I ask, giggling slightly as Baron tosses my naked body backward onto the bed.

"That, my darling, was my mouth on your cunt," he says, and I thrill at the sound of that word. *Cunt*. Hard, like the word cock. It was untoward—filthy—and I wanted him to say it again. But I'm distracted by his disrobing. Jacket. Cravat. Vest. Undershirt unbuttoned, exposing that dark, thick hair of his chest. His strong belly. When his pants slide off and his... cock... juts forward, I find myself swallowing. Licking my lips like I'm about to enjoy a splendid feast. Baron notices and then touches himself there.

"I want... your cock," I say, spreading my legs further, and Baron all-but-snarls as his face lands between my legs again. I jump, sensitive, but he's merely inhaling my scent. Inhaling and lightly teasing that bud with the tip of his tongue. I'm entranced by the look of his dark, curly head buried there, and after only a few moments, my hips are thrusting off the bed. Up into his mouth. Baron looks up at me, eyes dancing with mischief.

"My wife is quite greedy for pleasure," he says, nipping my hip bone, and I *am*. I want to be... to be filled somehow, and what he's doing isn't enough.

"More," I demand, chin tilted, and Baron arches a brow.

"As you wish, my darling," he says, crawling up my body, the hot, naked weight of him the most beautiful sensation I've ever experienced. He spits into his hand, reaching between his legs, head of his sex rubbing in my wetness.

"Will it hurt?" I ask, wrapping my legs around him.

The Gift

"A little," he says. "But I'll be right here with you, wife. Keep your eyes on my face."

I do, kissing him senseless, as his cock slides an inch inside of me. I am tight, so tight, but some muscle in me is opening for him. A bead of sweat drips down Baron's temple, and I want to taste it.

"More," I say, and he bites my lip playfully. Another inch. Another. There is pain, a stretching, but beneath that is a pleasure so rich it stops my breath. Baron continues that way, working himself in, and when he is fully seated, I am so full I can feel him in my throat.

"Tell me how you feel," he says, kissing my cheek.

"Happy," I say. "Filled with... filled with your cock." Baron's lip curls, and he moves out of me, just a little, and thrusts back in.

"Oh my *God*," I moan, the surge of pleasure unexpected. "What was *that*?"

"That was me fucking you," he groans then does it again—more roughly this time. My fingernails dig into his back, scratching.

"Do that again," I beg, and then for a while, we are unable to talk. Baron holds me down, drives between my legs, and it feels so good I am delirious again.

And then Baron rolls onto his back, taking me with him.

"Ride me, wife," he says, gasping, and my body seems to know what to do. Know how to seek and chase a second climax that is so close I can taste it. His thumb lands between my legs, pressing, and I throw my head back and *scream*.

There is no other worthy response—and I should have felt some embarrassment that our neighbors would hear me—but instead I embrace the ecstasy yet again. Embrace a feeling that has me bucking against my husband like a rider on a horse—

clawing at his chest and watching with joy as he experiences his own.

I am tender, and sore, but none of that stops me from pursuing my husband's cock for the entire night and well into the dawn. I take him between my lips and discover the power that comes from having a handsome man gasping on his back for you. He takes me from behind, and it makes me feel alive. In the morning hours, bodies exhausted, he puts his head *back* between my thighs, and I experience The Gift so many times I feel as if I'm levitating.

"Is this what marriage is like?" I ask, falling asleep on Baron's chest as the dawn sky erupts in pinks and oranges.

"This is what our marriage is like," he says, kissing my hair. Drifting off to sleep.

Although not an hour later, my dashing husband is rocking inside me again—the beginning of many, many gifts I would receive.

HE WAS LUKE SKYWALKER
(NOT HAN SOLO)

I can't believe Oliver is at this party.

He's standing there with a red solo cup, thick-rimmed glasses, and a messy mop of hair my fingers itch to run through.

And he looks about as nervous as I do.

Nerds like us aren't regular *attendees* at the frat parties. The room is hot and heavy with booze and dancing bodies and the kind of desperation college students wear like a cloak. But suddenly, watching Oliver attempt conversation with two drunk fraternity brothers, I'm no longer angry at my roommate for dragging me out here.

Even though I'm drowning in deadlines.

Even though the end of my senior year, with its daunting decisions, is just around the corner.

Instead I remove my jacket, trying to find a coat room, because my shirt is cute and I curled my hair and I'd very much like for Oliver to see it. We first met in freshman Biology —a class we aced. He sat one row in front of me, and I memorized the back of his neck, the fine hairs there, the careful way he took notes.

He'd smile timidly at me every morning, and over time, we talked more. Laughed more. He had a dry sense of humor, just like me, and a love of *Star Trek: Next Generation* (while I was more of a *Battlestar Galactica* girl).

He was Luke Skywalker, not Han Solo, and for the last four years, we'd taken the exact same classes. Aced the same labs, both on our way to pre-med. He felt called to help cancer patients while I was drawn to the heart—that bloody, ferocious thing that pounded like a herd of horses whenever Oliver blushed.

Or when he tripped over his words.

Or answered a question brilliantly.

Because Oliver was brilliant. And now here he was, outside of class, and as I hang my jacket in the small coat closet, I can hear his voice behind me.

"You're here," he says, shoving his hands in his pockets. A lock of hair falls over his eyes, and without thinking I reach forward and brush it back.

"I am. Didn't expect to see you here. Thought you'd be at the library."

He grins and reaches past me, grabbing a hanger. It brings his face close to mine, and he doesn't move away. "Library was lonely. I don't know. I've been in college four years and have never partied properly."

I shiver at his slight British accent, picked up from his London-born father.

"Really?" I ask and instinctively step back.

He follows.

"So you're here to study the mating habits of drunken seniors?"

He laughs softly. "It does seem a bit ludicrous, don't you think?" He indicates his solo cup. "Get yourself completely sauced, have sloppy, unsatisfying sex, forget in the morning."

A pause as he steps even closer. My back brushes against the jackets, light darkening.

"Unsatisfying?" I ask, quirking an eyebrow. "How can you prove that?"

Another soft laugh, huskier this time.

"Maybe I can't," he says, tilting his head. "But I just think sex is better when both people are passionate. You know. Fierce. Almost desperate for each other."

And then he reaches forward, cupping my face, rough palm against my soft skin.

I have fantasized about this moment for four years. His thumb traces my bottom lip.

"I'd have to agree," I breathe. "Although without empirical research, I'd have to say my opinion on hot, animalistic fucking is based purely on gut instinct."

Another step, and I am through the coats, against a firm wall.

"Is that so?" he asks, and he is leaning forward, ghosting his lips over mine. I try to capture his mouth, but he is teasing me. Keeping me waiting.

"That's my expert opinion, yes," I moan, remembering all the fantasies I'd entertained where Oliver rips my underwear in half and fucks me for *hours*.

In reality, we both hear the door close behind us. A jolting *slam*.

Oliver jolts, swearing under his breath.

"What was that?" I ask, but he is already at the door, investigating. He turns the knob to no avail. Again. A sliver of light shines through, illuminating his bespectacled face.

And a hint of mischief.

He turns, shrugging. A sly grin. "I think we're locked in."

"It's stuck?" I ask, still backed against the wall, still shuddering from the light brush of his lips. Oliver gives another hard yank, pounding on the door.

But the party's too loud, and everyone's smashed.

"Well," he says, ambling back to me. "This certainly gives us more time to finish our experiment."

He steps in front of me, sliding his foot between my legs, widening them. Reaches down, grasps the bottom of my skirt in his left hand.

"What's that?" I sigh. He drags his fingers up my inner thighs.

"We need some longitudinal data. A timeline. How long have these feelings been going on?"

With deft fingers, he slides my underwear to the side, thumb finding my clit. I suck in a breath.

"Yours or mine?"

He starts circling, slowly, softly, barely there.

"Let's go with mine," he groans, leaning forward to kiss up my throat. "The first moment I saw you, I thought you were a gorgeous mystery." His thumb speeds up but just slightly. He's kissing my cheek, my jaw. "Every class we shared, I was enthralled with what you said. The way you thought. Your calculations."

His lips find mine, and our first proper kiss is fucking *soul-searing*. When he finally pulls back, he slides two fingers into my cunt and hooks up, hitting a bundle of nerves that makes me black out for a moment.

"Fuck," I swear.

"My thoughts exactly." He grins, smoothly finger-fucking me, grinding his palm against my clit. He's watching me in total reverence, groaning at my reaction.

"All those years, I would fantasize about fucking you with my fingers. And now, in reality..." His fingers move even faster, and I drape my hands over the coat rack, rocking my hips. "In reality, I could fall in love with you like this," he growls.

I wonder, briefly, if I'm dreaming. But I can't be because, in the next instant, Oliver's on his knees, beneath my skirt, flicking the tip of his tongue over my clit like he's been studying cunnilingus techniques for *years*.

And, who knows, maybe he has because in a minute I'm screaming his name, my climax extraordinary and long overdue. He spins me before I can come back down, pressing me fully against the wall, and I love the *weight* of him. Love the feel of my skirt, bunched up around my waist.

Love the blunt head of his cock between the lips of my pussy.

He was Luke Skywalker (not Han Solo)

"And yes," Oliver says, breathing heavily. "I spent four years memorizing your face. The delicate arch of your neck. Your beautiful logic. You are so much smarter than anyone else in this bloody school."

There is the sound of a condom wrapper being torn open. A soft groan as he sheathes himself. He slides just an inch of his cock inside, and I arch my neck back.

"*More more more*," I moan, kissing him recklessly.

"You don't want to wait?" he teases, shifting one more inch. "Draw this out. See if we can't come to a different conclusion—" But my hero can't even finish his own sentence, instead slamming every inch inside of me.

I scream again and am rewarded with his long, ragged groan. He grabs my knee, bringing my leg up and open, spreading me.

Letting me take even more—and I do. I'm a quick study, after all, and he knows just how to fuck. Just how to rub my clit with perfect fucking pressure.

Just how to groan, over and over, that he'd been waiting for this moment for four long years. All of the jackets fall to the ground, the hangers come flying off the rack, and when we both climax together, we both release the same sound.

Of joy. Of pleasure.

Of sweet *relief*.

It takes more than five hours for a drunken sorority girl to finally unlock the closet, and in that time, we fucked and kissed and fucked and talked. I watched his face as he came, loved the slick feel of his cock in my mouth. I exploded in near-agony when he tongue-fucked me with expert precision.

And I told him about my medical school application—Boston, same as him.

"Boston, eh?" Oliver says in between licking my nipples. "Same as me."

"Yes yes *yes*," I purr, still sighing. "We'll see each other... we'll see each other..." but I trail off because he is kissing my stomach, moving lower, and is it possible to have seven orgasms in five hours?

"I hope we'll see each other every day," Oliver says. "Every day, every night, every weekend. And in every dark corner of the library."

He spreads my legs, settling there with a sigh of contentment. "Because I plan on making you come like this as many times as possible."

LIKE THIEVES IN THE NIGHT

I was pissed as hell that Lucas was there.

There was only one entry way into the bank—one *good one,* that is—and as I crept up to it, the shape of his stupid, giant body standing there filled me with fury.

Just once...

Just once...

"Just once I'd like to show up to a fucking job and not have you be here," I hissed, aware of security cameras and trip wires and booby traps as I stood, hand on one hip, the other pushing on his, well, very hard chest.

He looked down at it, like it was a bug he'd like to kill.

"How about you try moving more quickly *princess*? Then every goddamn thief in town wouldn't get the jump on you."

Anger blacked me out for a second, but the job—the hulking diamond on the other side of the bank safe—kept me semi-composed.

"Since I'd rather not go to prison for murdering you, I'll just remind you who 'got the jump' on you the last three times."

His nostrils flared as he took a step closer, almost backing me into the wall.

But I held my ground. Five years of this cat-and-mouse with Lucas. The thief community was tiny—everyone knew each other—and I'd hated him from the moment I laid eyes on his smug grin. I hated that stupid mop of gorgeous hair he was always pushing out of his perfect eyes.

And his voice...

I'd never heard a voice that just *sounded* like raw, urgent fucking. But this motherfucker had it.

Our unique skill sets were too complementary—we *were* always showing up at the same time for the same job. One of us was always going back empty handed after a battle of wills and skills.

But I wanted this diamond so badly I could *taste* it, wanted to hold a billion dollars in my hand and then wrench it from the multi-level, high-class security system I'd been studying for months.

"This is mine," he declared, pushing again, but I wasn't backing down. "I was here first. Playground rules."

I'd scoffed, a little too loudly, and his hand clamped over my mouth. Skin to skin, for the first time. Ever.

My first instinct was to drop-kick his ass, climb nimbly over his prone, sexy body, and have my way with that diamond.

My second instinct was unexpected: a searing lust like I'd never felt before.

"Do you *want* to get caught?" he'd whispered, so close to my face I could see those gorgeous eyes, the way his pupils darkened.

And he still hadn't moved his hand.

I pulled away though, angry and hot.

"Yeah I've spent a million goddamn hours of my life on this job just to get caught outside the door like an amateur."

Our faces were an inch apart, and we were both breathing heavily. Too close, too fast. A hint of that smug grin started to show, and my fingers itched to slap it off.

"Princess—" he taunted, leaning a centimeter closer.

"Don't fucking call me *princess*," I seethed, but then the lights flashed.

The wrong kind. The red and blue kind.

Lucas pushed me hard into the adjacent alley before I could even blink. So hard against the wall all the air rushed from my lungs. His big body covered mine, and his fingers moved back over my mouth. The lights flashed closer, I heard the scratching sound of radios, and my heart felt like it was about to slam itself right through my chest.

Neither of us spoke, eyes locked on each other, and what passed between that gaze weakened my knees—which pissed me off, again, since I wasn't a knees-weak kind of girl.

But it was lust and something else. It was that fraught understanding of what every professional criminal fears the most: being locked inside like a rat.

I wanted to run, and he knew it, trapping me against his body. And I felt it as the blue lights danced along the alley wall, harsh footsteps getting closer.

I felt his *cock,* massive and rock-hard, pressed against my pussy.

I spread my legs, almost imperceptibly, and he ground the head right against my clit. I opened my mouth and took a big bite out of his finger.

Lucas' lips *almost* snarled, but then he grinned again as he yanked his finger free of my teeth. The pulse in his neck was fluttering, I could see it. He was nervous too, afraid that the lights would swing down the alley, that we'd finally gotten caught.

No more cat-and-mouse chase from prison.

His fingers found my lips again, and he stroked them, lingering. A look of total adoration washed over his face.

"Princess—" he whispered again.

And then the sirens came.

"Did you compromise this job?" Lucas growled, the brief tenderness lost in the tension of the shrieking, screaming sirens.

"I didn't compromise *shit*," I said, trying to shift away from his hard body. But he had me captured against the wall.

"And what's the plan, Lucas? We're just going to stand here and let the cops come to us?"

"I don't know," he hissed, our faces close enough to kiss. The footsteps were moving closer. The bright glare of flashlights bounced off the street, the right angle of the alley, a lone dumpster.

We were deep enough that the lights kept missing us, but then we heard voices, distinctive ones.

Cops, searching for a person. Two people, at the semi-secret back entrance my source had sworn, up and down, no one else knew about.

A feeling of betrayal swirled in my gut. I was usually a good read of character. Had to be. It was why I hated Lucas on sight when we first met.

But I was trapped against a wall with him, the sound of his labored, nervous breathing in my ear.

I could hear the resonance of both our hearts, beating in a terrified rhythm. And the other thing demanding my attention, of course: his cock between my legs. Undeterred by the life-or-death situation unfolding around us.

The lights, the voices, came closer, and he flattened us against the wall, his hands pressed mine against the rough brick. When I met his gaze, it was like being punched in the gut: Lucas looked like he wanted to eat me *alive*.

One hand slid behind my back and down to cup my ass, pulling me snugly against his erection. Lucas groaned at the contact, and I fought to keep my eyes open as he started to rock against me.

"What in the ever-loving fuck do you think you're doing?" I whispered, feebly trying to inject as much anger in my voice as possible.

Tried and failed miserably. I basically *purred* at the asshole.

"You're doing strange things to me, princess," he whispered, and how could a man's *whisper* sound so much like sex?

Lucas lowered himself for the briefest of moments, grab-

Like Thieves in the Night

bing me round the thighs and pinning me against the wall. I was wearing thin, black yoga pants, and he kept dry-fucking my clit. I opened my mouth to tell him to piss off, but an honest-to-God *moan* slipped out instead. Lucas slammed his lips against mine, swallowing the sound of my pleasure.

Drinking me in.

Goddammit. Lucas shouldn't have been allowed to look that good and sound that good and *kiss* that fucking good. I was no longer aware of the sirens getting closer because the only sound I was aware of was his zipper sliding down. The crinkle of a condom wrapper.

His palm slid against my pussy, and I bit his lip, hard.

"Are you particularly fond of these?" he asked, gripping the thin fabric in his fingers.

"They're my favorite," I said against his lips.

And then he ripped them clean from my body.

"I wasn't fucking *joking*," I snarled. "God, you're such a—" but that sentiment was lost when he thrust his thick cock inside me. Tears sprung to my eyes because nothing ever hurt so *good*.

He bit my throat, fucking in a quick, desperate rhythm that had me clawing at his skin. He slid against my g-spot over and over, each time causing a sensation like a rising tidal wave, something terrifying and real that was going to break over both of our heads. I kissed him roughly, scratching at his chest, and the raspy, guttural sounds he made were going to haunt my dreams.

It shouldn't have been *possible*. I wasn't the kind of girl that could come this quickly, that intensely, but there I was. Screaming against Lucas's mouth as a climax ripped forcefully through my entire body. He came a moment later, eyes locked on mine, a searing gaze that made me whimper in recognition.

Nothing would ever be the same again.

The sirens and lights died away during our tryst, the heat off. I should've grabbed my tattered pants and ran. Never to look back. Hoping to God we didn't meet like that ever again. And I saw the same thought flicker across his face—we were cut from the same cloth, after all.

But he just stood there, staring at me instead of fleeing. His fingers linked with mine. Not perfect, not by a long shot, but who was in this goddamn crazy world?

"Come home with me," Lucas said.

And I did.

AMBROSE

I hadn't had a good man in a long, long while.

At thirty-two, I'd already been widowed for five years; my marriage to a fair-haired Earl (much older than me) ended as abruptly as a flame on a windy night. A carriage accident, a common death for a common man, and while I did miss him, I certainly did not *mourn* him. It had been a marriage of convenience in the truest of words, although his untimely death left me a sudden countess with a sudden wealth.

I was emboldened with independence.

But I hadn't had a good man in a long while.

Dinner parties, yes. Parlour dances, of course. The finest drink and food and company a woman could ever ask for.

Except that wasn't what I desired.

I desired to be fucked. Not handled or admired like I was by my recent gentleman callers. They were good for waltzes and moderately interesting conversation. That was all.

Specifically, I desired my gardener Ambrose. Barely twenty-one but big and sturdy with shoulders as broad as a house and rough hands with thick, muscular fingers. What was it about his fingers? I often found myself watching him from my bedroom window, on his knees in the dirt, wrenching and pulling and twisting. Asserting his dominance over my earthly estate. My gaze would linger on the dirt smearing his forearms, the dark red of his hair and beard, the planes of his chest sweating in the sunlight.

I'd sit and watch as my housemaid dressed my hair, crossing my legs to dull the ache that seemed perpetually there.

So I sent for him.

I lit a roaring fire and turned back the sheets of my magnificent bed. My hair was loose from its bun, and I was wearing nothing but my silk nightgown with bare skin beneath. Already I was slippery between my legs, imagining Ambrose there. In my private, erotic sanctuary.

Outside, the wind moaned, branches shaking their final autumn leaves. The fire popped and crackled, and my breath shortened with anticipation.

Was it wrong that Ambrose was so young? And a young man who looked like that must surely be betrothed to someone, some pretty girl in the village who looked at him with laughing eyes.

Maybe this wasn't going to happen. Maybe these months of yearning would be for naught, and I'd be destined to a cold, lonely—

"Lady Cecilia?" There was a knock at my mahogany door, sharp and to the point. I attempted to steady my nerves but remained seated by the fire.

"Enter," I replied. Watched the door swing wide, Ambrose's tall frame reflected in the flickering light. Hat in hand, Ambrose stared at me, defiance evident in the tilt of his bearded chin.

"You called for me, Lady Cecilia?" he asked with a voice deep as the ocean and rough as the sand on the shore. A lover's voice. The kind I'd want waking me from sleep.

"I did," I said, floored at my body's response to his nearness. He may have been young, but he was a solid, muscular, handsome man, and I wanted nothing more than to be ridden by him until dawn. "Come closer."

Ambrose strode into my room with more confidence than I'd ever felt at that age. Confidence and... curiosity. His green eyes roamed the hollow of my throat, the exposed skin of my ankles.

"I have a request for you this evening that I need to assess your... ability to perform."

Ambrose

He swallowed roughly, hands tightening on his cap. "Yes?"

"Are you betrothed, Ambrose?" I asked, sincerely expecting his affirmative answer.

"No, Lady Cecilia. I'm the last of my brothers to do so, but I've not yet found a girl that suits me."

Relief coursed through my veins. I was a lot of things, but a husband-stealer was not one of them.

"I'm sorry to hear that Ambrose," I said. "I'm sure one day you will make a girl very happy. You have... engaged in intercourse before?"

I expected a blush—a darting of the eyes—but instead Ambrose's gaze was pinned to mine with a knowing gleam.

Suddenly I was the one blushing.

"I've had a number of... lovers, yes, Lady Cecilia," he rasped, and my quim clenched in response. A twinge of jealousy, but I felt intrigue too: how had he done it? Taken them on the dirt in my own private gardens, skirts flipped up as he brought them to release?

"You're so young; that surprises me," I murmured, and he took a step closer.

"Not young like that," he said, voice barely above a whisper. "May I ask what I'll be performing this evening?"

Outside, the wind was howling, but the two of us were safe within this room. Safe. Private, removed from the view of prying eyes.

"Please kneel, Ambrose," I commanded because outlined against his breeches was a cock that had hardened impressively. It was quite possible that my handsome, young gardener had entertained erotic notions about me as well.

"I seek pleasure, Ambrose, and I'd like you to provide it for me," I said, uncrossing my legs and gliding the silk of my gown up the front of my shins until my knees were exposed. The hat dropped to the floor, and his chest heaved with a breath.

"And not a nice kind of pleasure," I continued, fabric caressing like a whisper past my knees, my thighs. A draft of air slipped over my bare quim. "A... harsher kind. Do you understand what I'm asking of you?" His eyes hadn't left mine, seemingly respectful.

Although the rapacious gleam there made my fingers tremble.

"That is my favorite type of pleasure, Lady Cecilia," he said on a low growl, and I knew I'd made the right choice for a partner. I settled my nightgown atop my hips, baring my sex to Ambrose.

"You may look now," I said, and when his eyes drank me in, he unleashed a raw sound. Emboldened, Ambrose leaned forward until his face was buried between my thighs and took a long, lingering inhale, the way he smelled the bouquets he picked from his garden for me each morning.

Another inhale, and I felt slightly delirious.

"Lady Cecilia," he said, giving me a broad, teasing lick. I gasped, attempted to close my legs, but his strong, coarse fingers grabbed hold of my knees and wrenched them wide. He shook his head at me. "May I confess a secret?"

We panted in unison beside a hot, roaring fire.

"Yes," I managed, entranced with his fingers stroking down my legs.

"The woman I'm waiting for?" Another inhale, another lick. Then his eyes, staring up at me from my most private place. "It's you."

It's you.

Of course. And then the many small signs of Ambrose's adoration sprang to the forefront of my memory: the daily bouquets of wildflowers. His eyes on my body as I strolled around the estate—an unending perusal.

And every time I'd speak to Ambrose, he'd stumble over his words, seemingly nervous.

Although there was no stumbling now.

His head was between my legs, tonguing my delicate folds with vigor. His eyes trapped me, and then he placed two of his fingers between my lips.

"Swallow, Lady Cecilia," he demanded. I did, utterly captivated. My heart was a restless, wild bird in my chest, and I feared levitation. His rough fingers were divine inside my mouth, the snarls of pleasure he made only spurring me on until I was rocking against the chair and taking his fingers as deep into my mouth as they could go.

"No more," he finally said, and those same slick fingers glided to my opening, clenching with need. Ambrose leaned forward and seared my mouth with a kiss that left me panting. Then he dipped inside my quim, sliding along the sensitive muscles until the pad of his index finger found a small button deep inside my body.

"Do you know what this is, Lady?" Ambrose asked, kissing along my neck as my eyes shuddered closed.

"N-no, I don't," I admitted, canting my lips forward, seeking his hand. His finger moved in erotic circles against the bud, stimulating the tight blossom of my pleasure, causing it to unfurl and open at the base of my spine. Ecstasy came alive on every nerve ending from the tips of my fingers to the top of my head.

"It's the center of a woman's pleasure. Her secret." Another kiss then teeth grazing my jaw. "Although I've found yours. Your secret is greedy, Lady Cecilia."

"Yes, *God yes*," I panted, rocking myself shamelessly against my gardener. With a devious glint, he lowered his lips again and brushed them against the tight bud at the top of my quim. Another button—and the two being worked in tandem sent me spiraling into a euphoria so strong I cried out. I wailed, hips shaking, legs shaking, lungs shuddering with every breath. And through it all, Ambrose watched me dutifully from his knees, talented hand working betwixt my legs.

"Am I performing well, Lady Cecilia?" Ambrose asked, lips curved in a half-smirk, but I reached forward and cupped his length through his breeches.

The smirk vanished like smoke.

"I... I cannot," he groaned, firelight caressing his handsome face.

"Cannot what?" I taunted, fingers loosening the fabric and freeing the full, heavy length of his cock. We both watched as my fingers slicked up and down, the head fat and shining. I had been *so long* without a good man, and I was half-compelled to worship at the altar of this magnificent body part.

"I cannot be teased like this," he said. But I kept going, wanting to wring pleasure from his body—harder, faster, my fingers wet with his arousal.

"I think you like it, Ambrose. I think you want—" but the words were barely out of my mouth before he grabbed my wrist. Stilling my motions.

"Was I not requested for a specific service, my lady?" He glared although his lips twitched at my cheeky smile.

"Well done," I purred, kissing him gently. Licking between his lips and wrapping my legs around his waist. A sweet, sensual exploration of his body occurred: off came his shirt and breeches and undergarments, baring a body that was hard-worked and muscular and dotted with freckles. With one arm, he clasped me about the waist and hurled me to the ground roughly.

"You wanted harsh, correct?" he asked, thumb stroking across my lips. I nodded once more and watched his expression turn feral. With a snarl, he wrenched my knees wide and positioned himself at my core.

"Please..." I sighed. "Please please *please*." His big hands held my waist, lifting the lower half of my body off the floor.

And then he thrust every inch of his cock to the hilt.

I screamed, no longer concerned with anyone hearing me during this dalliance. I wanted to be ridden, and Ambrose performed, giving me quick, forceful thrusts that had my body sliding across the floor. Bending over, he lifted my chin and took my mouth, timing his tongue with the movements of his cock. I was mindless with pleasure, my climaxes beginning and ending, breaking like waves against the shore. With a growl, Ambrose flipped me onto my belly and took me that way as well, groaning huskily against my ear, using words so filthy my toes curled. Slamming himself against me without cause or dignity, the two of us making sounds like animals. Clawing at each other, scraping and biting. Near the end, he reached forward and grabbed a handful of my curls and pulled my body up to meet his—his chest to my back. Fucked me in short, rapid strokes until I was screaming again and his teeth were clamped onto my shoulder. In the mirror, I watched Ambrose reach his own crest—face gorgeously unraveled as he chanted my name.

Lady Cecilia, Lady Cecilia, Lady Cecilia.

By the fire, the two of us dozed and fucked. He gave me everything I'd ever wanted in a man—gave it to me until my skin was bruised and tender and entirely sated.

And all through the next day I wore a secret, charmed smile that refused to abate. As did Ambrose when I spied on him from my bedroom window. When evening fell, draping my estate in darkness, I sent for him.

"Am I needed to perform your services again this evening,

Lady Cecilia?" Ambrose asked, hat in hand and standing in the doorway.

"You performed... quite well," I said, legs crossed by the fire again. "I was pleased."

With a nod, he approached and dropped to his knees again. I gave him a long, lingering kiss—and when I pulled back, he was beaming at me like a man in love.

"May I perform them for you again, my lady?" he asked, fingers already sliding beneath my gown.

"You may," I sighed, settling back in my chair and spreading my legs.

THE WEDDING

1

DIEGO

I was stuck in the bachelor party from hell.

Not from an outsider's perspective. No, an outsider would exclaim at the marvelous white sand beaches of Cabo San Lucas. The turquoise waves. The silky, sultry breeze. My best friend Jeremy had decided to give himself an all-expenses-paid bachelor party in paradise. The two of us. Our friends from college. His brothers.

And Levi.

That's what made it hell.

I hadn't seen Levi in five years, but when Jeremy told me he was inviting our former college roommate and favorite friend Levi to be part of his wedding party, I pretended to be enthusiastic. Levi had been living on the west coast since we'd graduated, and his absence had been felt dearly—for Jeremy because he thought of him as the quintessential third leg of our triangle. Three best friends. Roommates. The person we shared poignant college memories with. Wild parties. Hellacious hangovers. Road trips and finals and late nights in the library.

The difference being that Jeremy hadn't spent all of college *in love* with Levi.

But I had. Had even, the night before we'd graduated, semi-drunkenly declared that love to Levi. Who'd only smiled sadly and pretended he hadn't heard.

And it was fine. Really. I'd had my fair share of boyfriends since then. So had Levi if Facebook was accurate. Not that I looked him up that much on Facebook.

Okay, I looked him up on Facebook *all the fucking time.*

And he'd only grown sexier. Levi Tanaka. San Diego surfer. Human rights lawyer. Rescue dog owner.

In the five years since I'd seen him, the pining had only worsened. And now we were sitting next to each other on this white sandy beach at a dinner celebrating our best friend, and all I could do was think about how good he smelled.

"Diego," he said softly as soon as he'd sat down. He was wearing a white linen shirt, half the buttons open, exposing a chest as smooth as I remembered. No shoes, pants rolled up past his ankle. "How are you?"

I paused, holding a tropical drink halfway to my lips. I wished I'd had more of these before this fateful meeting, but I was sober and sunburned and not at all prepared.

"I can't believe you're here," I said, eyes locked on his. We'd never, ever, spoken about what I'd said the night before we graduated. But I thought about it constantly. "Did you... I mean, how am I? You're the lawyer with the dog and the cute—"

I stopped myself, blushing lightly. His lips quirked up.

"Someone's been doing their homework," he teased. "And it hasn't been that long. Only five years. Feels like yesterday, right?"

I took a swallow of too-sweet, mango-flavored liquor.

The Wedding

"Um... sure," I managed. "And you didn't answer my question."

"Was it a question? I thought you just said, 'You're the lawyer with the dog and the cute...'" His head tilted, thinking. "Cute what?"

"Boyfriend," I said, the mango liquor loosening my tongue. "Right? The guy you've been posting recently?"

Might as well just dive face-first into embarrassment.

Levi looked away, briefly smiling to a friend across the table. The mood was jovial, light. Reggae played softly behind us. And Jeremy looked ecstatic. Also drunk.

"Oh, he's not my boyfriend. Anymore," Levi said with a shrug. "I broke up with him right before I came here."

"Why on Earth would you do that?" I asked. The guy had been hot. They'd looked like two male models together, posing for a GQ ad.

"I just didn't want..." he trailed off. Shifted in his chair until our knees brushed together. Just once, but it was enough to send blood surging to my cock.

"Want what?" I asked. The twilight cast Levi in its periwinkle glow, and all my heart could do was beat furiously. I'd missed this man. Yearned for him. Pined for him. And in person, it was only worse.

His eyes locked back on mine, an expression I couldn't quite read. "Because I thought this trip might have a lot of temptation."

I almost choked on my tropical drink.

"What does that—" I started to say, but then we were interrupted by Jeremy tearing his shirt off and racing into the water. The two of us burst out laughing on instinct.

"I can't believe, of the three of us, that crazy son of a bitch is the first one to get married," I said, grinning as he splashed naked through the waves. A few other bachelor-party guests were starting to join him, carrying drinks into the water as they shed their clothing.

Levi shook his head. "Do you remember when we road-tripped all the way to Miami?"

"Slept in the car," I mused, a shock of a memory hitting me.

Levi and I both asleep in the back. Me, waking up early, watching the early-morning sun glide along Levi's perfect, sleeping form. He'd woken, very briefly, and for a split second, I'd thought he was going to kiss me.

"I puked in that bar on the beach, remember?" Levi smiled, leaning closer to me. "And you got in that fight."

"Wasn't a fight," I laughed. "Merely... a heated, drunken argument."

From the waves, Jeremy yelled our names. "*And you better get in here with your clothes off, you bastards!*" he bellowed, and I let my head drop into my hands.

"The night has barely started," I sighed. "We should start pulling together bail money right?" I turned, but Levi was standing up, unbuttoning his shirt right in front of me.

"I believe we have instructions," he said lightly, but there was an intense gleam in his eyes that stole my breath away. "Are you coming?"

One by one, Levi slowly undid the buttons of his shirt, eyes on mine the entire time. The moment felt completely still, unbound by time, like five years of secret, private fantasies come to life. There was his smooth chest, the tan skin, and ridge after ridge of hard muscle.

I'd dreamt about those muscles. In my fantasies, I'd tongued every one, categorized the various moans and sighs I'd wrench from Levi's throat as I pushed him to the edge. And now, in front of me, it was almost too much.

"Diego," he said quietly, unsnapping his pants. His hip

The Wedding

bones were carved by the gods. "Are you just going to stare, or are you going to join me?"

"Where?" I mumbled, in awe as his pants dropped and he was left in tight, black briefs. It was impossible to miss the thick, hard length of a cock I'd thought about constantly.

"Into the ocean," he laughed, a quiet rumble. He ran his hand through his hair, looking like a male model, posing in the sand. A real-life fantasy, beckoning me into the ocean.

"Diego," he said again, voice raspy with desire. "You want to come, don't you?"

2

LEVI

I was here to seduce my former best friend.

It'd been a long five years, and I thought fleeing to the West Coast and dating a bunch of beautiful men would help me get over my feelings for Diego. But I had no chemistry with those beautiful men, and really, there was only one man for me.

Diego. And those feelings didn't wane in five years, only steadily grown stronger like flames roaring through a field. An endless path of destruction.

When Jeremy invited me to his wedding, it was either decline and let those feelings consume me or go and see if Diego felt an ounce of what I'd experienced in college.

"You want to come, don't you?" I asked, reveling in the feeling of the warm ocean waves, lapping at my heels. The salty air on my bare skin. And Diego staring at me the way a starved man stares at a meal. His throat worked, eyes lingering between my legs, and I was half-tempted to stroke myself for him, right there. But we were surrounded by people, and really, I'd always thought of seduction as an elegant affair.

Although my lust for Diego was anything *but* elegant.

The Wedding

"Yes, I mean... um, yeah," Diego said, tripping over his words, and his blush was as cute as I remembered. Diego had told me he'd loved me once—black-out drunk the night before our graduation. I'd ignored it because he wasn't in the right frame of mind and I never thought he meant it. But now, watching him strip out of his shirt right there on the beach, I could feel the yearning emanating from his entire body.

I raked my eyes over Diego's dark skin. Swallowed a growl when he kicked away his shorts. I could make out the outline of his cock, thick and heavy, and I grew even harder.

"Do you remember when we skinny-dipped on that road trip?" I asked, keeping my distance as he walked into the water next to me. Jeremy was yelling and jumping in the waves ahead of us.

"Of course," Diego laughed. "Yet another time when I swore we were going to get arrested."

"That was the theme of college," I said. "The thrill of almost getting arrested."

Diego smiled at me, and I let our shoulders brush together. The night was luxuriously steamy and so fucking lovely.

"So how are things with you?" I asked. "With your life?"

Diego arched an eyebrow. "Want me to sum up the last five years?"

I shrugged. "It's strange, I know. Going from talking every day. To... well, never."

Diego looked away for a second. "I've really missed you, Levi."

I didn't trust my voice not to crack, so I side-stepped his admission. "And how have the last five years been? Honestly."

"I'm an ASL interpreter." He smiled, and I nodded with recognition. Diego's little brother was born deaf, and Diego had always wanted to do something to help the deaf and hard-of-hearing community. "And I love it so much."

"That makes me incredibly happy," I sighed, loving the look of contentment on his face. "It's good to love your job. To love your life."

Diego pinned me with a curious glance. "There's a lot of things I love about my life. One thing missing though."

"What's that?" I said, voice still light as a feather. The waves were a little rougher farther from the shore, and Diego stood closer to me than I could handle. Water beaded down his chest, and he smelled like mangos.

"I never really met someone," he said. "Dated plenty but... no one who caught my fancy."

"You're picky," I teased, and he laughed a little.

"Not picky," he clarified. "Just waiting."

There was a heavy pause between us, and I wanted to kiss him senseless in the middle of the ocean. A wave crashed against our hips, knocking me against Diego's hard chest. Immediately his hands wrapped around me, steadying us.

"Whoa," I laughed softly, lips close to his. "Thanks for saving my life."

"That's a major over exaggeration," Diego laughed. "But I'll take it." Neither one of us moved away, content to hold each other.

"Did you miss me too?" Diego asked, too sharp to let me get away. His cock was hard against mine, and he ever-so-subtly rocked his hips. A gentle thrust, but I couldn't help the shudder that moved through me.

"Of course I missed you," I said roughly, feeling vulnerable in the water. I was supposed to be seducing Diego, not the other way around. "I thought about you... often," I lied, since it was really every day.

Another subtle drag of his cock against mine, and my eyes

The Wedding

closed for a second. It could have been an accident. It could have been the waves. It could have been anything... except it was *Diego*.

"I thought about you often too," he said. Our lips danced closer, and this time I thrust against him. Harder. His jaw clenched.

And then Jeremy crashed into us, wild with laughter.

3

LEVI

After Jeremy ruined one of the most sensual moments of my entire life, the mood on the beach shifted. From quiet seduction to drunken hilarity, and before I knew it, we were out of the ocean and Diego was putting his clothes back on... which was not part of the plan.

I growled in frustration as we walked toward the hotel bar, eyes snagging on the broad lines of Diego's back. He'd thought of me. Which I'd hoped to hear, the many nights I dreamt of Diego. I used to entertain this specific fantasy: coming home to my lonely San Diego apartment and finding him there. Cooking in my kitchen, a wry grin on his face. A domestic moment. A sweet moment.

A dirty moment—because in my fantasy, I'd walk in, and he'd tilt his head. Hide his sweet smile, replace it with a scowl. Snap his fingers, and I'd be on my knees, posturing before a king.

I thought about Diego's cock in my mouth so much I worried I'd developed a compulsion, and as he sat across from me in the bar, sipping his drink lazily, I wanted him to snap those fingers.

The Wedding

Who knew, really? Maybe Diego wasn't the aggressive, controlling lover I thought he'd be. In college, he was the Nice Guy. Charming, funny, kind-hearted. Quick to laugh. Five years later, and he was still that, but I sensed something hungry shifting beneath that façade. Something that would make me work for the privilege of his pleasure.

"You okay?" Diego asked, startling me from my reverie. "You look distracted."

I shrugged, letting my eyes wander the bar for a moment. Snagging on a couple at the end, so clearly in wild, passionate love, I couldn't help but look. The man was a giant, some kind of Viking from a past life, with long hair and a thick beard. His partner was pretty and inked, lavender-haired and laughing.

"Look at those two," I said, indicating the pair. They were laughing and sharing a drink, flirting easily. "They must be on a honeymoon or something."

Diego watched them for a second, grin on his face. "Maybe not. Maybe they're just always that fucking in love with each other."

I chuckled. "Diego the romantic. Is the guy your type?"

His eyes stayed on mine. "He's handsome as hell. But I have a different type."

I swallowed roughly. "Interesting." Our knees brushed together, and I leaned forward, letting my palm land high on Diego's thigh. If anyone looked, we were just two friends, locked in intense conversation. "Back home, do you take a lot of men home from places like this?"

He shook his head. "I don't do the stranger thing. Never could. I've always had boyfriends."

A hot spike of jealousy—maybe I would end up being the dominating one after all. I didn't like the idea of Diego dating, even as I knew that thought was ridiculous. I'd left the day after we graduated. He was free to do as he pleased.

"But you didn't... fancy any of them," I said, remembering our conversation in the ocean. "Not even a little?"

"Not even a little," he said, widening his legs ever so slightly, causing my palm to slide up a half inch. I could feel his thigh flexing beneath my fingers. Another three, four inches, and I'd be able to wrap my fingers around the delicious length of him.

"I'm sorry to hear that," I lied, and he smirked, just a little.

"Well, I have to say," he started, laughing nervously. "I was always a little jealous of your boyfriends."

"Really?" I asked. "Why?"

"You just... seemed so happy and in love. I always thought I'd find that, but it didn't feel that way to me. Not passionate enough."

I nodded, fingers moving one more inch. "What kind of passion are you looking for?"

4

DIEGO

My name was Diego Alvarez, and I was officially about to become the first person to ever orgasm from thigh-touching.

Ever since Levi had rubbed his stiff, hard cock against me in the ocean, I'd been one nanosecond away from climax. For a number of reasons—most notably that it was becoming more and more obvious to me that the man I'd pined over for almost nine years might... might... *might* feel the same way about me.

That and the fact that Levi was the sexiest man I knew and definitely the sexiest man in this heated, tropical bar right now. Linen shirt still unbuttoned, a naked chest that begged for my tongue, abs that rippled in a way I'd only ever seen on male models. All of that plus his sly grin and wandering fingers dancing up the side of my thigh.

"What kind of passion are you looking for?" my former best friend asked me, and now the entirety of his palm lay inside my thigh. Squeezing. I felt every connection, every place his skin touched mine.

"Oh, you know," I said nervously, attempting to avoid his

gaze and failing. This couldn't be happening. This was like some fever dream I was trapped in, and any second I'd wake up to my dog licking my face.

"Diego," he pleaded with his dark brown eyes. "Tell me. Tell me what you want in a partner. Or a lover."

I fought fainting. Managed to stay upright. Levi's palm slid higher, tips of his finger just grazing my cock. One stroke, and I would be coming in this bar, in front of everyone.

And maybe that was what Levi wanted.

"Excuse me for a second," I said, standing upright and searching for a bathroom. Or a hallway. Or someplace I could get some air. "I just need... I'll be right back."

Concern flashed across Levi's face, but he didn't press. "Um... okay," he started to say slowly, but I turned on my heel, heading toward the back in hopes of finding some relief. It was too much, too soon—the thought that Levi might feel the same way I did. Because I didn't really know where to go from here. I had no plan, just feelings.

So many feelings.

"Diego," I heard Levi call behind me, but I was already yanking open a bathroom door. I waved him off, but instead he caught the door. Wrenched it open. Squeezed in behind me and slammed it shut.

It was small, and we were pushed up against each other just like in the ocean. Except this time Levi had me boxed against the wall, both hands on either side of my head. He was breathing heavily, almost angrily, and when he thrust his erection against mine, I hissed out a breath.

"What are you doing?" I panted because he was doing it again. I didn't know what to do with my hands, and they hung by my sides in tight fists.

"I'm pretty sure you know what I'm doing," he growled, lips hovering over mine. "I feel like you spent all of college

The Wedding

wanting to take me. And I spent all of college wanting to be taken. And now I'm here, and you won't do a fucking thing about it."

"I didn't know," I said, desperate for his mouth. "I didn't know, okay?"

"Then you're an idiot," he said and then crushed his lips against mine.

I had a switch. Or that's how I thought of it. Deep inside me, and it was almost never tripped. Even with countless lovers, it tended to stay on the soft side. The easy-going, submissive side.

It wasn't a side of myself I explored often. Because really there was only one man I suspected would bring it out in me.

Levi, of fucking course.

His lips met mine, and in a second, I backed my best friend against the wall. Hard. Gripped his face and held his mouth hostage. Took Levi like he'd wanted to be taken. Owned him. Claimed him as my own. Tongues and teeth. Firm lips and low, masculine growls. I hooked his leg up and dry-fucked him roughly, grinding our cocks together until he was a panting, useless mess. Putty in my hands to play with as I pleased.

"Oh God, oh God," he groaned, and I sped up my motions. Fucked him as hard as I could, cocks rubbing, lips joined together. It felt like heaven and paradise and goddamn ecstasy all rolled into one. The two of us, stuck in this tiny bathroom, hands *finally* on each other.

"That's not the name I want to fucking hear," I hissed, snapping my hips as Levi shuddered. "You know what I want." He was close, I could tell—desperate, raspy moans tumbled from his lips. I slid down his zipper and grasped a cock as thick as I'd always imagined. Gave it two powerful strokes.

"Diego, Diego, Diego," he chanted, head back against the wall. Mindless now—so quick to please. So eager to come.

And just when he was balancing on that edge, I stopped. Gave him a brutal kiss and pushed him to his knees.

The sight of Levi, my love, my everything, on his knees like that? Well, it was almost too much for a man to take.

Except for the way he looked up at me in that moment, flushed and sexy and handsome as sin.

And then he fucking smiled.

5

DIEGO

Levi. On his knees. Palming my straining cock as if it was the most beautiful experience in his entire fucking life.

Was this real?

"Am I dreaming?" I asked, briefly breaking the moment, my control. I honestly couldn't tell. But Levi shook his head and kissed my palm sweetly as I stroked his hair.

"No. You're not dreaming, Diego," he said. "I'm about to suck your cock until you drench my throat." With deft fingers, he slipped out my cock. Stroked it—just once—and my eyes rolled back in my head. "This feels real, doesn't it?" He leaned forward, sucking my balls into his hot, hungry mouth.

"Fuck," I said, a brutal word. "Fuck, that feels real." Another suck, his groaning sounds, fingers dancing along my length. Then his mouth moved lower, my shorts yanked down, cheeks spread. Tongue licking and tasting along the tight ring.

"What the actual fuck," I hissed, fighting back to the ledge of my sanity to regain control. His fingers were still stroking, tongue searching, and I was reduced to just nerves and sensation.

"Take your cock out," I bit out as sternly as possible. Levi stopped, looking up at me obediently. Stripped off his shirt to reveal those delicious abs again. Slid out of his shorts and gripped his thick, bobbing cock. "Stroke it."

He did, letting out a strangled gasp, and then he took all of me to the back of his throat. I thread my fingers in his hair, holding him there.

"I didn't tell you to stop touching yourself," I growled, and his fingers worked between his legs, the moans deep in the back of his throat vibrating through me. I loosened my fingers, and he took the cue, beginning to work me over with those full lips of his.

"Such a dirty fucking mouth, Levi," I said. "Who would have thought? You were always so good in college. So fucking nice." He locked his eyes on mine and swirled his tongue expertly. My vision darkened at the edges. The walls pulsed with sound and music, lights flickering, but I only had eyes for Levi.

"I want to see you come while I fuck your mouth," I groaned, pushing him back slightly. Resting my hands against the wall for leverage. He tilted his head back, and I thrust my hips into his hot, wet mouth. Levi was stroking himself roughly, grunting around my skin as I slid between his lips. I wanted to fuck his mouth. I wanted to fuck him, thought about taking him on his hands and knees. How beautiful he'd be, the way he'd shudder and cry out as I fucked us into oblivion.

"God I've thought about this for so long, you have no idea," I said, laughing painfully as my hips moved. "Every night sometimes. It's like a *compulsion*." I was panting, and Levi was groaning, and then his finger slid between my ass and right inside of me. Pressed on that bundle of nerves so perfectly that fireworks exploded across my brain.

The Wedding

"It's too good," I begged, giving up any semblance of power to my best friend on his knees. "You're too amazing I can't... I'm not sure I can hold out..." I was fucking his lips erratically now as the muscles of his stomach shook and strained. He was the man I'd loved since I was nineteen years old, and suddenly he felt too far away.

"Up," I said, stilling my movements. "Fucking stand up."

6

LEVI

It's like a compulsion.

The five years I'd been apart from Diego had felt just like that—a presence in the back of my mind, half regret, half curiosity. What if I'd said something to Diego when he said he loved me the night before graduation? What if I'd kissed him in the back of the car when we were on our road trip? Would we be together now? Would my life be happier?

What if. What if.

"Fucking stand up," Diego growled, yanking me from the most beautiful place I'd ever been: on my knees with every inch of his delicious cock between my lips. But then he wrapped his arms around me in a passionate kiss, a battle of tongues and teeth, a searing brand. Our cocks brushed against each other, and I shuddered in his embrace.

"I want to be inside you more than anything in the world," Diego said, wrapping his strong fingers around my length and tugging. My head tilted back.

"Look at me," he snapped. I did.

"Do you understand that, Levi? More than *anything*. I've

The Wedding

been dreaming of fucking you for five years, but I can't—I won't—just take you in this goddamn bathroom."

"Please," I begged, grasping his shoulders. "I think we should." I was so needy around him, a live-wire of want.

"No sweetheart," he said, lips on my jaw, my neck. "Not like this. Not our first time. But I need you to touch me." Another jerk of his fingers. "Like this."

I moved quickly, grasping his cock and groaning into his mouth. "Come with me, Levi. I know you want to," he rasped. I nodded, barely coherent. The rough sounds of his pleasure, the slick sounds of our moving fingers, our sloppy kisses—it wasn't going to take long.

His movements sped up, a blur of motion, one hand gripping my face. He conquered my mouth, even as I felt his body shake with exertion. We couldn't stop kissing, couldn't stop needing each other.

"Oh fuck fuck fuck," I panted, kissing him harder. Jerking him harder. I looked down at our cocks together, our palms, our fingers. Diego's palm. Diego's fingers. At the base of my spine, an orgasm threatened to destroy me.

"I'm so fucking close," I managed to grunt. Plead, really, and then was granted with Diego dropping gracefully to his knees and sucking my entire length to the back of his throat. One swirl of his tongue, and an orgasm rushed through me. I cried out, pumping between the wet paradise of his lips, and looked down to see Diego coming with his own fingers, groaning around me.

Leaning back on his heels, head against the wall, he looked up at me, panting. Grinning. Wet lips and come on his fingers.

"What the actual *hell*," I managed to say before falling to my knees and pressing my lips to his. That same kiss from earlier, only deeper this time. Soulful and sweet, the lingering eroticism of our encounter in the taste of his tongue, the tiny sparks of awareness as his fingers caressed my throat.

"Levi," he asked, finally breaking away. "Is it okay that we didn't fuck in here? I just... I don't want you to think that I didn't want it. Or you."

I grinned, smoothing his hair. "You made it pretty obvious how much you wanted me," I said. "And yes." I kissed his cheek, beneath his ear, breathing in the scent of his hair. "Plus, I'm curious what you had in mind for our first time."

"You and me. A hotel bed. A Do Not Disturb sign on the door. Maybe some champagne. A giant box of condoms and a Costco-sized bottle of lube."

I chuckled softly and pinned him with a gaze. "I'd like that."

There was a pounding on the door, shaking us from our reverie. And then Jeremy's drunken voice: "I know the two of you are in there, and I hope to sweet fuck you are finally fucking because, dudes, I've been waiting for this for years—you were so fucking obvious in school—but, you know, I'm also so drunk I think I might die? And can you please help me? Please?"

We both laughed, and I yanked open the door to see a horribly sick-looking Jeremy, lilting against the door. "You look like you fucked niiiiiiiiiiiiice," he slurred, trying to give me a high five and failing.

"And you're getting married tomorrow and are a complete goddamn wreck," I said, pulling Diego up off the floor. "Good thing we're here to get you sober."

7

DIEGO

Things I had done since Levi and I had put Jeremy to bed with Gatorade, Aspirin, and promises of greasy burgers in the morning:

1. Not sleep. At all.
2. Think about how I'd sucked Levi's cock and it was better than five years' worth of pining and fantasy.
3. Not fucking sleep.

And now the two of us were standing in tuxes as Jeremy paced, looking nervous and excited and slightly nauseous all at once.

"You need another burger?" I asked, reaching out to steady him for a moment. But he only shook his head, flashing a grin.

"I feel amazing, dudes," he said. "I think getting married is the ultimate hangover cure. I'm serious. All the adrenaline. That and the fact that I'm so fucking in love with my future wife I can't stand it." He pulled the two of us in for a sudden hug. "And now the two of you are finally banging? God can this day get any better!"

We were saved from further embarrassment when the photographer came to snap him up for a few extra photos, leaving Levi and me finally alone with about fifteen minutes left before the ceremony.

"So uh... I guess we didn't really hide it too well back in college, huh?" Levi asked, blushing a little in a way that made him alternately sexier *and* more adorable.

"Guess not," I agreed. "Come to think of it, I might have been almost black-out drunk, but was Jeremy in the room when I, um, when I..." Even with last night's intimacy, I couldn't seem to say the words "confessed my love to you" right here, right now, at a wedding and wearing tuxes with the sun shining and flowers blooming.

"Probably," Levi shrugged. "He was always around. He even would tease me about it, when you were in class. Said I should stop making moon eyes at you and just go for it."

I swallowed roughly. "Just took five years, huh?"

"Worth it," he said, eyes on mine. "Worth every second." Levi looked around discreetly and glanced at his watch. Then gave me a devious smile.

"How long do you think it would take you to come right now?"

"Whaa—" I started to say, but Levi was already tugging me into the small closet near the ceremony area. We went from bright, beach-y sunshine to total darkness.

Darkness... and Levi's body pressing mine to the wall.

"I didn't get to return the favor last night," he said against my lips, kissing me savagely.

"I thought that was for tonight," I gasped, head back as his fingers deftly freed my cock from my tuxedo pants. I was already hard and halfway there because that's what happened when your soulmate drags you into a supply closet for a quickie blow-job.

The Wedding

He gave me three long strokes, and I groaned loudly.

"Shhh," he admonished, fingers on my lips. "And tonight I'm going to let you fuck me for hours, however you want." Another perfect stroke. "Tonight, you can use my body however you'd like to. Because I'm yours." Levi was jerking me off now, panting as quickly as I was, and I couldn't stop touching him. Arching into him. Completely undone even though I was supposed to be the one in charge. In control.

"You'll be lucky if you can fucking walk tomorrow," I managed to growl and was rewarded with Levi dropping to his knees again, just like last night, and sucking my cock so deeply all I could do was come—spectacularly—with an orgasm so immediate it shocked me. I drenched his throat, and the greedy sounds of pleasure he made dragged an after-shock of ecstasy right through.

"What the ever-loving *fuck*," I gasped, half-falling down the wall, but Levi's strong hands caught me.

"I stayed up all night thinking about that," he said, kissing my cheek. My jaw. Down my throat. Tucking me back inside my pants—no one would be the wiser. Because he'd swallowed every last drop of my come.

"And now you need to smile and act like a normal groomsman and *not* like you just had your cock sucked in a supply closet," Levi laughed, giving me a sloppy kiss and slipping through the open door. "Come on, handsome. They're waiting for us."

And with a tug, I was back in the sunshine. Staring at a gorgeous beach, down a long, sandy aisle, shoulder-to-shoulder with a man I'd imagined marrying a thousand times since the first day of freshman year when his earnest grin just about knocked my heart into the next stratosphere.

"You ready?" he asked, and that's when the strains of the wedding march started up.

8

LEVI

"Can I have this dance?" I said, striding up to Diego, man of my dreams. We'd smiled and laughed and gotten slightly choked up during Jeremy's ceremony. Had danced and been photographed and stuffed our faces with cake.

But now I just wanted to hold his body against mine in the soft ocean breeze.

"You know how to dance?" Diego teased, sliding his fingers into mine. I gave a hard tug until he was flush against me. Wrapped my hand around his lower back and kissed his fingers.

"I know how to do a lot of things," I said against his ear and was rewarded with a shiver. "And I've been thinking about our hotel room tonight. How about you?"

Diego shifted, and I could feel the hard ridge of his cock lined up right against mine. I growled, nipping the skin along his throat.

"I don't know. I haven't really been thinking about it." He smirked and gave me a kiss. "And can I ask you a question?"

"Absolutely," I said, twirling us toward the center of the

The Wedding

floor. Behind us, Jeremy and Abigail danced outrageously, half-drunk and in love.

"Why didn't you say anything? The night I confessed my love to you?"

His voice was rough with tension and longing, and when I pulled back, there was sadness in his eyes. Sadness I had caused.

"Diego," I started, and he swallowed roughly.

"Just tell me the truth," he said, shaking his head. "If you spent four years pining for me the way I pined for you, you could have said it back. We could have spent the past five years together instead of apart."

We swayed on the dance floor, lips close together, hearts pounding in beautiful synchronicity.

"I have no excuse, just apologies," I finally said, sensing the delicate tight-rope we now walked. We'd exhausted our first night of pent-up lust together, but these confessions were something else entirely. Honesty. Integrity.

Love.

"You came to me that night beyond blacked out. Slurring your words, about to pass out. I put you to bed, watched over you. Made sure you were okay," I said, remembering that night with crystal-clear clarity. "And yeah… every hour or so, you'd say something along the lines of, 'Levi, I love you so fucking much.'"

His cheeks tinged pink, and I pulled him closer. "Which was adorable and made me want to dance through the streets. But you were so drunk, and I truly hadn't thought you'd felt the same way. Guessed that I was alone in my yearning and worried I'd…"

"What?"

I gave a sheepish grin. "Confess my love to you and have you reject me. Tell me it was a joke. And that would have ended everything. Our friendship, our trust. So I fled to the West Coast like a coward because, when I realized how deeply I loved you, I knew we could never be friends again. Knew I'd just spend my entire life in love with someone who didn't love me back."

Diego pressed his lips to mine, soft and sweet like ripe peaches on the first hot summer day.

"You're such a fucking idiot," he finally said once I was gasping against his mouth. Because even sweet Diego had the ability to send sparks racing along my spine. "And I'll forgive you if you tell me the moment you first realized you fell in love with me."

I grinned, twirling us around the floor. "That first night we met, we stayed up late talking. You made me laugh so hard— you just got me. What I loved. What I was interested in. And you were so kind. Kind and... so good. You're so good, Diego. The best person I know. I just remember us sitting on our dorm floor in bean bag chairs, half-stoned and a little drunk, and you looked so fucking sexy. Hair tousled, laughing, shirt riding up so I could see your hipbones." I was getting hard at the memory, all the youthful exuberance of that night. The deliberate lust. Wanting to claim his mouth with mine but holding off. Denying myself.

"I remember that night," Diego said shyly. "I thought we were going to kiss."

"Me too," I said, pressing our hands together. "When did you first realize you loved me?"

"That blow job in the supply closet two hours ago," he said, and I threw my head back and laughed.

"Keeping it a mystery, eh?" I asked as the song slowly ended. The night was tapering off, couples pairing up and heading to hotel beds for sweaty, sultry sex. Something I very much wanted us to be doing right now.

The Wedding

"Maybe I'll tell you later," Diego said, dragging his lips up my throat until they caressed the shell of my ear. "But first? I'm going to take you to my hotel room and fuck you until you can't stand." A bite of his lips and a subtle rock of his hips. "Get ready to confess your love all goddamn night."

9

DIEGO

We were a blur of frenzied, erotic motion. The moment I placed the Do Not Disturb sign on our hotel door, I had Levi up against it.

"Everything off," I ordered against his gasping lips, tearing, ripping, tossing, throwing. There was no more time for games. No more foreplay. No more teasing.

I was going to fuck Levi tonight.

"Should we open the champagne?" he managed to grunt as I licked my way down his abs and took the length of his cock into my mouth. Naked, he was glorious. Naked, he was the light of my goddamn life. The man I'd been dreaming of since I was a stupid freshman and he flashed me that grin. The one that made my heart feel like it was going to beat right out of my chest. "And, *oh fuck*, don't stop doing that."

"You don't get to give the orders," I growled, sliding up his hot body and all but shoving him onto the bed. I lifted his arms above his head, twisting our fingers together as I ground our bare cocks together. "And you are the most beautiful goddamn thing I've ever seen."

"Diego, fuck," he hissed, arching his hips against mine,

The Wedding

seeking greater friction. "You feel so... that feels so..." And I almost let him come like that, our chests pressed together. Hands bound. Hearts beating as one.

But I had plans for Levi. Plans five years in the making.

"On your stomach, sweetheart," I said, eyebrow arched, and he dutifully complied. He was gorgeous, all tan skin and lean, hard muscle. I took my time, licking up the backs of his thighs as he shuddered. Bit the juicy flesh of his ass. Spread him so my thumb, and then my tongue, could swirl around his tight, clenching muscle. Levi groaned against the sheets, a raw, masculine sound that had the hair standing up along my skin. That had me pray, fervently, that we could stay like this—hot and urgent for each other in the slick dark of this hotel room. On the edge of climax, clawing our way toward release.

"I want you ready for me," I said, tongue swirling inside. He almost wailed, and I grinned, loving his response. Loving that I was the one responsible for his pleasure, his gasping release. His hips flexed against the bed, and I gave him a ringing slap.

"No cheating," I admonished, dribbling lube onto my trembling fingers. I turned him, needing to see his face, and slid two fingers inside his ass.

He practically shot off the bed, fingers fisting the sheets. And I stayed there on my knees, watching his cock jutting forward, abs flexing. Throat exposed, head back, groaning with raw ecstasy. Stretched and slid my fingers, wet and slick, until I had driven him mad with desire.

"Levi look at me," I said, sliding a condom down the length of my cock. I fisted myself for him once, and he bit his lip. Hungry. "I've waited a long, long time for this moment."

"Me too," he said softly, and I took his lips in a sweet, searing kiss. I notched my cock at his entrance but didn't move.

"I fell in love with you the night before we graduated," I said, sliding inside just an inch. Just a tease. Swallowed his moan with my mouth. "I thought I had a crush on you. An attraction. Something vapid and fleeting." I slid in another inch. My vision started to darken. "But that wasn't it at all. It was love. Pure and simple. And all-consuming." I flexed hard and bottomed out inside of Levi. For a moment, the two of us could only press our foreheads together, breathing tightly. I was aware of every sensation—his ass squeezing my cock. His hard dick pressed between us. His smell. His taste. His shuddering sighs.

"And I was really fucking scared you didn't want me back," I slid all the way out, then slowly worked my way back in. Enjoying Levi's ragged groan. "Thus the black-out drinking and the confession of love." Another thrust. Another. Our lips hovered together, and I wrapped my fingers around his cock. Gave him a delicious tug.

"I wish we'd realized then, I wish..." he started, but he was moaning too loudly. And so was I, my mouth pressed to his shoulder as I flexed my hips against his ass. Took him in a punishing rhythm that had me moments from climax.

"It's okay," I whispered against his ear. Knowing he was close. "It's okay. This is us. This is beautiful. This is perfection." And then we were nothing but a tangle of sweaty limbs, poetic motion, two men in love searching for the same release. Our lips stayed together, Levi's fingers digging into my back, and as I raced toward the edge, Levi came—beautifully.

I joined him not ten seconds later, and ten seconds after that, Levi had the superhero ability to stand up, open the bottle of champagne, and pour a splash of it onto my stomach.

"Hey," I laughed, attempting to turn away but powerless to his curious tongue, licking up the sweet and bubbly liquid. "I

The Wedding

just professed my love to you, fucked you into oblivion, and now you're pouring alcohol onto me?"

He sat up, took a generous swig, cheeky look in his eye. "It's a celebration, handsome."

"Oh yeah?" I said, sitting up on my elbows. "And what are we celebrating?" He pressed his lips to mine, and I tasted effervescence.

"I mean, probably when I get back from this wedding, I'll have to quit my job, sell my house, and move out here. Right?" A slight blush—he was nervous. "So I'm just pre-celebrating all of those major life decisions."

I dragged him on top of me where he settled comfortably. "Hey," I said, thumb stroking his cheek. "You'd do that for me? Move back home?"

"I only moved there to get away from... from this," he said. "From wanting someone I thought didn't want me back. But now..." His smile blossomed, the warmth of it hitting me like a ray of sunlight right to my chest. "What am I waiting for?"

"What are we waiting for?" I said softly as he laid down, head nestled against my shoulder. "We've only been waiting since college."

A soft laugh, a sloppy kiss. "I say we've got a lot of lost time to make up for."

ANOTHER BORING NIGHT AT THE OPERA

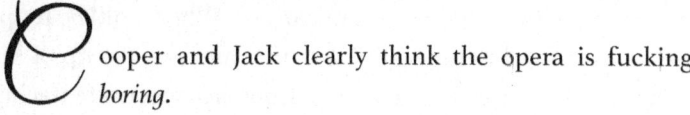ooper and Jack clearly think the opera is fucking *boring.*

And quite frankly, so do I.

For the first hour of the show, I had two, devilishly handsome men—looking dapper as hell in their tuxedos—with their hands placed innocently on my knees. Then slightly above my knees. Then my thighs, gliding smoothly, dangerously, toward my hips. The singers on the stage could have torn their clothes off and danced a jig while juggling tiger cubs, and the entirety of my attention would have remained locked on their hands. Stroking and teasing and doing what they do best.

Setting me on fire.

A round of applause explodes around me, and Cooper leans over me to straighten Jack's tie, pausing to swipe his thumb over his full lips. Jack tosses me a wink when he catches me watching. Because he knows I *love* watching. And when Cooper starts to lean back, he brushes his fingers over my breasts. Quickly. Just his thumb, sliding over my nipples.

I hissed in a breath.

Jack places his mouth against my ear and breathes against it—no words, not yet. Which is good because Jack's words have a tendency to make me orgasm. On some nights, Cooper and I fuck spectacularly to Jack's filthy instructions.

Sometimes he even films us.

"You wore this dress on purpose, kitten," Jack whispers as the opera singer throws her hands wide, hitting a note so high I almost wince. I shake my head, and Cooper's fingers slip under the hem of my dress.

"You did. Because you wanted Cooper and I to be tempted to rip it *the fuck* in half and suck on those pretty nipples until you come in front of these opera patrons. Who would be properly scandalized at the sight." A pause, and just the tip of his tongue grazes my ear. To my right, Cooper's fingers are tracing intricate patterns on my inner thighs. "You're lucky I have so much control," he semi-sighs as if suddenly regretting that control.

I'm regretting it as well, almost painfully aroused by the thought of climaxing just from nipple play in front of these people. Jack's fingers are stroking the back of my neck in the same maddening pattern Cooper is tracing on my thigh.

I bite my lip.

"Don't," Jack whispers. "Don't bite your lip like that. Only I get to do that."

I stop.

His fingers move down my neck to my collarbone. "I bet I could slide my hand even lower," he says and does it. "See? No one's even looking." His hand dips into my bra, grazing my nipple, and Cooper's fingers press against my clit through the fabric of my underwear. That's all they do—a beautiful, choreographed dance to get me off.

This is my life with them.

The lights flicker up for intermission, and their hands disappear just as rapidly. Clearing his throat, Jack adjusts his jacket while Cooper brushes a fleck of dust from his cuff links. Relaxed. Confident. Almost smug. And as the fancy opera patrons stand up, I watch multiple sets of eyes flicker over my men in clear admiration. Jack places a warm hand on my low back, guiding me forward with a possessive strength. At the bar, Cooper sips whiskey, neat, looking like a dream. He catches both Jack and I watching and winks.

A blush works its way across my cheeks—which still surprises me since earlier this week he'd fucked me so hard I

Another Boring Night at the Opera

couldn't sit down for two days. It's the beautiful duality of my men. Jack's filthy-mouthed but fucks me sweetly. Reverently. Worships me like a goddess, prone at my feet.

Cooper, my golden-haired surfer boy, winks at me like a high-school crush, holds my hand as I step around puddles.

And fucks like a savage animal, finally unleashed.

Together, they are insatiable. Together, we can't be stopped.

"So here are my thoughts kitten," Jack says, hand still on my back. Cooper tosses the rest of his whiskey back, locking eyes with Jack. A silent communication passes between them.

"We could keep watching this boring-as-fuck opera," he says, dark eyes growing darker. "Or we can find the nearest closet, and Cooper and I can take turns fucking your delicious pussy."

There was a heavy pause—bodies were all around us, draped with diamonds and white gloves. The sound of polite laughter sparkled like crystal on glass. And next to me were my tuxedoed heroes, looking handsome and impeccably dressed, even as they promised to devour me.

"Your choice kitten," Jack says with a crooked grin. "What will it be?"

I mouth the words *fuck me*, and the next thing I know, they're dragging me into the nearest closet so quickly I almost laugh.

But the pained looks on their faces stop me.

Jack kicks the door open, shoving Cooper and I inside, and before the door is even fully closed growls, "On your knees. Get her wet, but don't let her come."

And now I can really let go since Jack is in charge now, leaning against the wall and already stroking his cock as Cooper slams me against the wall. Yanks my dress up to my hips, drops to his knees, and eats my pussy with abandon. My eyes are locked on Jack, watching us with such a keen hunger it's all I can do to not beckon him over.

But he likes to wait, likes to let Cooper and I dance together before he joins in.

Cooper's talented tongue has me coming apart in minutes, and that's when Jack stalks over, slapping a hand over my mouth and dropping his lips to my nipples. I bite his palm, trying to smother my screams, and with a hiss, he yanks Cooper's head back, beckoning him upwards. Suddenly I'm between both of them, mouths coming together, my pussy juices smeared across Cooper's chin. Jack's teeth graze my neck, then he kisses Cooper passionately. I am trapped between two hard bodies, two hard cocks, and I reach down to stroke both, loving the heady power. Loving the groaning sounds they make as they kiss.

Cooper grabs Jack's face and there is so much love and yearning there my heart *aches*.

But they haven't forgotten about me. Suddenly, it's Jack on his knees, licking my clit in awe, whispering against my skin. His tongue is gentle; Cooper's fingers are mean, pinching my nipples between his thumbs. Twisting. My orgasm lingers at the base of my spine, ready to make itself known, but I've denied myself with them long enough to know how to hold off. To let the sharp arousal burrow beneath my skin, becoming part of me.

And I'm proud of myself as Jack's tongue moves more quickly, as Cooper's fingers continue to pinch and torture. But then the head of Cooper's cock notches right at my entrance, and his hard thrust claws a scream from my throat. His hand slaps over my mouth, and he is gripping my shoulders, yanking me onto his cock, and Jack is feathering his tongue over my clit, and I am *gone*.

Another Boring Night at the Opera

Floating-through-space-*gone*.

I don't so much come as explode, trembling with the shock of it, in love with the sounds my beautiful men make as they deliver my ecstasy.

"Just like that, kitten," Jack says, stroking my thighs. "Let go for us." Cooper is grunting behind me, usually so fierce and stoic when he fucks. But his whispered "You're perfect," is so sincere tears spring to my eyes.

Until then, he bends me in half, continuing his hot, furious thrusts, and I take Jack's cock into my throat as deep as it will go. Wrap my hands around his waist to steady myself, letting Cooper's thrusts push me onto Jack's cock.

I can't see now—I am nothing but scents and sensation, a body being taken apart by two greedy lovers. But I hear Jack's growling moan and Cooper's panting breaths, and one of them—I'm not sure who—is circling my clit. The closet is nothing but masculine grunts and bodies slapping together, and it is so fucking hot another orgasm crashes over me.

Jack comes in my mouth, drenching my throat, and I swallow every drop as he strokes my face tenderly. Holds me against his chest as Cooper continues to fuck me, his movements erratic now. Jack's tongue tangles with mine as I lean back against Cooper, loving the feel of his hands on my breasts. Jack kisses Cooper—hard—and that's when he comes apart against the two of us with a curse and a cry. He is so magnificent, blond hair in his eyes, cheeks flushed with euphoria.

And later, as the three of us sit through the final, third act of the opera, it is with secret smiles and relaxed, happy bodies. Content and warm. Just three patrons, enjoying a night of art and song.

Except not thirty minutes after we've fucked wildly in a

closet, Jack and Cooper have their hands on my knees again. Then my thighs. Then my hips.

And I know it's going to be a long night.

SEIZE THE DAY

*T*he student in my Poetry 301 class is the most beautiful woman I've ever laid eyes on. Dark, luxurious tresses that tumble down her back. Midnight eyes that flash. A sexy smirk—because she knows I watch her, have *been* watching her, ever since she strode into my class in tight, ripped jeans and a tank-top that read *Carpe Diem Motherfuckers.*

Seize the day. She wore it often, as if taunting me into action. Taunting me into doing the thing I said I'd never do.

Fuck a student.

Because, yeah, the other professors did it. My student Eva is almost twenty-one years old, and although I've just turned forty, the age gap feels nonexistent. Because her stanzas shock me to my core. They are raw and rough—broken shards of sea-glass that glisten in the moon-light. Dangerous but appealing. Eva is a siren on the rocks, and I'm every sailor in existence. It conceals her younger age, and at night, as I read her stark, vibrant couplets, my nerve endings sing with pleasure.

I just don't know if she's attracted to me—another woman.

I feel eyes on me often enough to know that a fair number of my students find me sexually attractive. But Eva is a mystery —her smirk possibly part of her overall act, not an invitation for me to spread her long, lithe legs and dive into the sweet mystery of her cunt.

But I want to, and as class ends and the lights dim, it's just Eva left in the room. Eva looking suddenly shy—for the briefest of moments—before steeling her spine and approaching my desk.

"Professor?" she asks, sliding her hip onto the ledge of my desk, staring down at me. I am captivated by her hair and have to fight a primal urge to sift it through my fingers.

"Do you have a question, Eva?" I ask.

She bites her lip, glancing back at the open door.

"I do. Well, a proposition really," she says. "But if you take it the wrong way, it'll... it'll make class a lot more awkward. Or, conversely—" one distinguished brow lifts, "—it'll make class a lot sexier."

My breath stills as I lean back in my chair, crossing my legs. Eva lets her eyes roam my body.

There is a carnal hunger there.

My nipples are tightening against the thin silk of my top. Eva notices.

"Is what you're about to ask me terribly inappropriate?" I ask, also aware of the open door. Our voices are soft, and if any person walked in, we'd appear as professor and student. Nothing more.

"It is," Eva says, sliding closer. Up onto the desk until she is sitting, knees closed, directly in front of my body. "But all the great poets of our time seized moments like this. Life. Need. Want." Eva licks her lips and slowly, slowly, widens her legs. Beneath her skirt, her pussy is bare and glistening.

My hands tighten on the chair, but I hold her dark, lovely gaze.

"You're propositioning your teacher because you think it's going to give you inspiration for a poem?"

Eva shakes her head. "I'm propositioning you because I can't stop thinking about you. Because I've fucked a lot of women, Professor, but just your eyes on me in class is hotter than all of it. Every time, when I leave, I walk back to my dorm room. Lock the door. Slip beneath the covers and—"

I reach forward, driven by some poetic, artistic desire to inhale her scent. She gasps as I yank her roughly to the edge, spreading her legs forcibly. I take a moment to simply breathe her in—the musky, earthy smell of her. The unique smell of

Eva. Lips wet. Clit beckoning. The heady, erotic rush I always got between the thighs of a beautiful woman.

"You know someone can walk in here at any moment, right?" I say before closing my teeth along the skin of her inner thigh. She yelps. "So you'll need to do two things for me, pretty girl."

"What's that?" she asks, eyes shining. Fingers stroking my cheek.

"Stay absolutely quiet," I say, giving her clit a long, flat lick. She doesn't moan, but her entire body seems to shimmer. "And come when I tell you to."

"I'm not sure I can—" she starts to say, but then I let my tongue dance an intricate, swirling rhythm against her clit, and she slaps her own palm over her mouth to quiet a wail. We were fucked either way if someone caught us, so I let any semblance of appropriateness drain from this moment in time.

I shove my student back until the entire length of her gorgeous body splays across my desk. Head falling off the side, her long black tresses scraping the floor. Eva's back arches and writhes, her breath in short, panting gasps, as I lick her clit in a steady, demanding rhythm. Slide two fingers inside her wet pussy, allowing myself the softest groan at the way her muscles clamp around my fingers.

So greedy.

So sweet.

There were footsteps and voices and plenty of times when I thought we were going to get caught—which only spurred me on. Made me lick her faster, harder, her fingers tangled in my hair. My other hand slid beneath her shirt, palming her breasts, her nipples. I can't stop looking up at her, wanting to burn this experience permanently into my mind. I wanted this moment for poetry, for literature, for daydreams—this gorgeous woman with spread legs and my face buried between her thighs. Body writhing on my desk. I was as close to climax as I'd ever been, and as my beautiful Eva wailed against her palm in release, I circle my clit roughly and orgasm—sharp and bright with my tongue still buried inside of her.

We weren't caught, and afterward Eva left on shaking legs, hair mussed and breathing unsteady. I went home with a smile that wouldn't leave my face—captivated by my student.

The muse I didn't know I was looking for.

And of course, a week later, my dark-haired goddess stops by my office again. Propped the door open as wide as it could go. Slowly lifted her shirt over her head—a daring, public strip tease.

"What's your proposition this time?" I ask, leaning forward to lick the edges of her hipbones. Eva dropped to her knees, eyebrow raised, and spread my legs.

"Extra credit," she says with a smirk.

SHE'LL ALWAYS KNOW THE TRUTH

*Y*ou're fucking *tired* of everyone thinking you're the Nice Guy.

The goofy singer with a penchant for acoustic guitars and sweetness. You know what They Say. You know what your reputation is—and it's a fine one.

But it's not the truth.

You are spending all day twirling a gorgeous woman around a ballroom for a music video that any critic would call "romantic." But your hands on her waist aren't romantic. Neither are your fingers in her thick, apple-red hair. The two of you have flirted all day, in take after take, her skirt flying through the air and giving you the most delicious glimpse of the paradise between her legs.

Every time the camera's rolling, you go farther... press your fingers more tightly. Nuzzle her neck. Let the barest hint of your lips graze her ear. She feels it, too—breathing hitched. A flush along her collarbone.

You are not the Nice Guy. Beneath that acoustic-guitar-demeanor beats the heart of a man who would do anything to get a woman off, the filthier the better.

And it must be sheer serendipity that leaves you and your gorgeous dance partner alone in the ballroom that night—the sudden quiet almost startling. No techs, no cameras, no makeup artists. Just you and her... still dressed in that white dress, hair wild around her face.

She knows. She'd been picking up on your dominant signals all night, and you can barely fight a grin as she steps primly toward you. Crosses her wrists behind her back and sinks gracefully to her knees. Eyes up—wide and watching.

"Hello gorgeous," you say, stroking her under the chin. This entire day felt like long, drawn-out foreplay.

"I want to play," she says, opening her lips for your willing fingers. She sucks them, eyes bright.

"I don't play nice," you say softly, verifying her interest. "Are you okay with that?" She nods, whispers her safe word. You store it away, lean down, and give her a sweet kiss.

It is the last time you'll be sweet.

Using your fingers, you pry her jaw open, release your straining cock. You smile, a little, when her brows shoot up at the size of you. Your dance partner lunges forward, and you let her—taking note of her tight nipples, pressed against the sheer white of her top. The glimmer of wet between her legs. And then your cock is enveloped in wet, hot, sucking heat, and you snarl. Your fingers twist in her hair, pulling hard, and tears spring to her pretty eyes.

You don't mouth-fuck like a nice guy. You take her throat with a viciousness, spurred on by her abject pleasure. She purrs and moans endlessly, hips thrusting off the floor, fingers straining behind her back. She wants to touch, but you deny her. Instead, you continue to fuck into her mouth until you are mindless with need.

There is something else you want. With a groan, you stop her ministrations. Grab her by the throat and haul her back onto the ground. With strong fingers you tear her white dress completely in two until she is sprawled out in front of you, gloriously naked with shreds of fabric clinging to her skin. Her head is facing you, tipped back, and it's all too easy for you to crawl over her body. Her mouth lands on your cock again—greedily—but your lips are now on her clit, and with one suck, she is half-screaming around your length.

The two of you are writhing bodies on the hard ballroom floor. Still fully dressed, you fuck her mouth and lap at her clit and twist your fingers inside her cunt. This is what you live

She'll always know the truth

for: the Not-Nice Guy. It's not that you're into sex with strangers because you're heartless or a commitment-phobe.

It's just that fucking, to you, is everything. The sounds, the pleasure, the raw, pulsing need. Slapping skin and panting breaths and bite marks and the delicious thrill of a tongue along the curve of an ear.

You want to fuck strangers because you are insatiable, and the more pleasure you can bring to women, the better. If a person could be addicted to that, then you surely are—addicted without a hope for reform.

Your dance partner comes. Once. Twice. Before the third, you roll onto your back, keeping her on your face and holding her there as your tongue continues to explore every inch of her pussy. And later, it's all too easy to tear off your tie and shove it into her mouth. Blindfold her eyes with the palm of your hand. Fuck her in long, frenzied strokes on the ballroom floor. Your climax has you biting her neck like an animal, and she screams around your tie.

Months later, you can't watch that music video without getting hard. So romantic. Ethereal. A ballroom dance between a lovely couple.

Only the two of you know what happened after.

And your dance partner comes by sometimes—always submissive. Always ready for you to be Not Nice.

She'll always know the truth.

LET IT BE YOU

I was sitting cross-legged on the floor of my bedroom, staring open-mouthed at the boy I'd fallen in love with when I was eighteen years old.

Except he's no boy anymore.

It'd been four years since we last saw each other, and the only thought that seemed to ricochet through my brain was *holy growth spurt*.

The last time I saw Patrick, we were breaking up, tearfully, after spending a hot and heavy summer together before college. But he was headed back to Cork, Ireland, his home, and I was off to UCLA. It was for the best, really, but after I'd seen him off at the airport, I'd cried for weeks.

And spent four years at college missing him.

I didn't tell a single soul because, deep down, it was silly... yearning for a boy I'd only spent three months with.

But Patrick was gentle and sweet—a poet at heart, with brown, soulful eyes and a mop of curly dark hair that I loved to run my fingers through. A shy, crooked smile and that Irish accent that makes my body tremble.

Seeing him four years later, I began to realize those feelings were *more* than just yearning.

And Patrick was no longer a floppy-haired poet.

The person sitting cross-legged on the floor with me was a *man*. A thick-shouldered, lean-waisted, deep-voiced man.

A man telling me that he was still a virgin.

"Start over," I said. "Tell me again."

His smile crinkled the corners of his eyes. "I graduated from Cork, got my Literature degree. And now I'm getting my Master's at UCLA. So I live here now." His accent lilted like petals in the wind.

"Congratulations," I said. I remembered being eighteen

and talking endlessly about school. He had always been studious, a deep thinker. Intellectual.

"And," he continued. "In the four years since I last saw you, I've not had sex with anyone. I'm a virgin." Patrick reached forward for my thighs. Gave a tug until our knees touched.

When he said the word *virgin,* a swift bolt of arousal struck between my legs.

"What did... I mean, what *have* you done?" I asked, tongue-tied.

He shrugged, eyes twinkling. "Same things we did the summer before I left. I dated a bit while I was back in Cork. And with those girls we did... oral. Fingers, hands." A slight blush in his cheeks, and for a second, Patrick looked just like he did that summer, picking me up for a date.

But then I focused on his words, and the images they evoked in me were *scandalous.* I expected to feel jealousy that his lips and tongue and fingers had touched other women. Except all I could remember was his shy, hesitant tongue, exploring the folds of my pussy the first time he'd ever gone down on me. How I'd encouraged him, showed him the way, and when that tongue had given me an exquisite orgasm, my blushing boyfriend had looked anything *but*.

Predatory.

Confident.

Almost... smug.

I thought about his dark, curly head between the legs of countless Irish girls at Cork, bringing them to release, and it felt like my own private, dirty movie.

"What have you done, love?" he asked. I squirmed beneath his gaze.

"I lost my virginity a few months after you left," I said, biting my lip. There is hurt, and some jealousy, in his gaze. But also *interest*. I wondered if he was thinking the same thing—imagining another man's body moving over mine.

Both of his palms landed on my bare knees, and I was oh-so-aware of it. "It didn't mean... I mean, it was fine. And while it was happening, I thought about you."

I'd fantasized about his body, the feel of his cock between my lips.

Patrick clenched his jaw. "And what happened when you did that?"

"I came," I said. His fingers slid all the way up my knees and onto my inner thighs. "Will you tell me why you didn't lose yours?"

He laughed softly, looking away. I wanted to run my tongue up the side of his neck. "I guess I was waiting for you."

It took barely a moment for me to lean forward and kiss him. And it felt like *everything*: teenaged nostalgia and hot nights and the sweetness of a summer romance.

But then Patrick slid his tongue between my lips, and the delicious ache between my legs roared to life. I'd missed kissing him—oh how I'd missed it. Four years of pining feel like *nothing* compared to the fierce urge I had to take him inside my body.

"Rosie," he said, sighing as I wrapped my legs around his waist. "I want it to be you. Please let it be you—" but I was already rocking against his erection. Nipped at his jaw and tore his shirt over his head. Patrick had lean, hard muscle and dark hair on his chest.

And when I freed his erection, his breath shuddered against my ear.

I reached up, fingers opening my bedside drawer. Drew out a condom. The two of us were still on my bedroom floor, grinding against each other. As I opened the condom, his thumbs grazed my nipples.

"What do you think it feels like?" I asked, pushing him to the floor. Off came his remaining clothing, and before me was a veritable *Adonis*. Tan brown skin, midnight hair, thick muscled thighs. I leaned down and bit a ridge of muscle, and he groaned. Teased his long, veined cock with my tongue before slowly, slowly rolling the condom down.

"Wet," he said, watching me lift my shirt off. Remove my bra. "Hot. Tight." I slid my underwear down my legs, and I was naked in front of him. Patrick growled, a real growl, and he was no longer blushing or shy.

His back arched off the floor, head back, neck exposed. The sound he made was so rough and real and *sated* that I almost came. I worked my cunt down, then up again, his fingers bruised my hips.

"What the ever... loving... sweet... *Christ*... fuck..." he groaned, lifting me and slamming me back down. I was enthralled with his response, wanting him to direct and move my body the way that he craved it.

"What does it feel like?" I asked again. I rode him smoothly, licked his throat. Nuzzled his ear as he lost his mind beneath me.

"Paradise," he sighed, flexing his hips up and then rolling me onto my back and driving his cock home. Then it was my turn to arch and moan, staring up at him in pure wonder. He was part poet, part animal, and his lips on mine was pure worship.

"You are perfect and beautiful, and it was worth waiting four years for this. It was worth waiting for *you*, Rosie."

I grasped his shoulders, and his thumb stroked my clit. I jumped, startled, and then Patrick worked his thumb in small, steady circles. Just like I'd taught him, years ago. We were both rushing toward the edge.

"Come with me," I whispered, lifting my legs higher on his

body. Taking him deeper. His strokes became faster, unpolished. He was unraveling before me, and I was drunk on it. And it was his climax—his first climax inside a woman—that sent me hurtling toward orgasm. We spiraled and leapt and broke free together—a glorious, sweaty, happy mess on the floor of my bedroom.

Later, I took Patrick to the Santa Monica boardwalk where we drank cheap beer and ate tacos and reminisced about the summer we'd once spent together. He told me stories about Ireland and read me poetry and confessed he was nervous about his degree.

The sun set over the ocean, turning his hair copper, and our feet touched in the cool sand.

"What happens next?" I asked, warm and content by his side.

Patrick grinned at me, the four years apart melting away. "I think I take you on a proper date. How does that sound, love?"

CUFFED

1

WILL

I wanted to lick every inch of Violet D'Allegra's long legs. From my vantage point across the restaurant, I watched her cross those legs once, twice, three times. And each time I fought a dark urge to drop before her in supplication.

This was the fifth night in a row I'd tracked her here, and it always started like this: she'd arrive before her mark, find a table, and order a glass of chilled white wine she'd never drink. She'd take out her phone and scroll through, ignoring the stares from other men in the room. Her fingers would trail along her collarbone, the edges of her dress, drawing the eyes of her many admirers.

It had an effect, one that I was about to see in person. Her mark had arrived. Jack Peterson was easily fifteen years her senior and one of the wealthiest venture capitalists in San Francisco.

Well done, Violet.

I watched him look for her, his gaze finally landing on the table far in the back. I saw the hunger in his eyes.

She had it too. They just never saw it.

I noticed every subtle movement of her body. She knew he was here, though to a casual observer, she looked distracted, even bored, with her phone. With one hand, she tossed her long black hair over her shoulder, exposing her beautifully bare throat. She crossed her legs, again, and I swallowed a growl. Under the table I could see her fiddling with a gold ring—the only sign at all that she was nervous.

Jack made his way over, and as casually as I could, I moved further down the bar, bringing my beer with me.

"Everything okay, sir?" the bartender asked.

I ignored him, too focused. I couldn't hear what Jack said, but she looked up, tilted her head, then let a wide, smoky smile light up her face.

I first thought it was the smile that got them. It was the kind of smile a naked woman might give you as she stretched out on your bed with her hands above her head. It was a smile that promised. A smile that delivered.

Like all predators, Violet knew how to snare her prey. The smile was the beginning. Standing up was the ending.

She'd worn The Dress. Black, tight as sin, with a slit damn near up to her hips. Violet D'Allegra had the body of a 1950s pin-up model, and that dress should have been illegal. The spike heels she wore showed her mark she was sexy and spontaneous.

The dress, her heels—they were her weapons, wielded carefully.

He was a goner.

Jack was easier than most, and he folded like a paper napkin.

I drank a second beer and watched their date. If I angled myself just right, I could see her face, watch her expressions. She laughed at everything he said, letting her fingers trace her collarbone, the strap of her dress sliding down her left shoulder. At one point, she reached forward and grabbed his arm, then pulled back, blushing.

The perception of innocence was important to Violet.

My phone vibrated with a text message that I ignored. I knew who it was.

If she succeeded tonight—and the signs were good—he'd fuck her soon. I used to feel pity for them, even a self-righteous anger. Now, I seethed with twisted jealousy.

But it really wasn't a good idea to fuck the woman you were also desperately trying to arrest.

My phone vibrated six more times, enough that I knew I'd be in deep shit if I didn't pick up soon. I left Violet and Jack and stepped outside into the breezy San Francisco night.

"What?" I snapped.

"That wouldn't be the tone of voice I'd take with *my* boss, but we all make our choices, I guess."

I leaned against the wall and rubbed my forehead. "I'm sorry, sir. Having a rough day."

"Will, we're all having rough days. Especially since I have two pompous millionaires halfway up my ass, demanding answers. Which, interestingly enough, is why I'm calling *you*."

I'd been tracking her for two months now, from San Diego up the coast of California and now San Francisco. To her marks, she was Violet D'Allegra. In the office, we called her Man Eater (and sometimes much worse). Real name: Unknown.

Her deal was seduction, blackmail, and theft—or so we thought. So far, all we had was the testimony from two men—one from San Diego, one from L.A.—who claimed Ms. D'Allegra had taken them for one hell of a ride.

Violet had done her research carefully, seducing powerful, wealthy men in loveless, but politically important, marriages. Her marks cried "blackmail," but when we pushed them further on it, they locked up fast. They wanted something to be done without their own involvement. But without further evidence, they looked like two idiots who'd gifted large sums of money to a mistress then regretted it.

Even after she'd ruined their lives, Violet controlled their silence. I wasn't sure how.

The only reason I'd been put on Violet's tail was because my sergeant was eyeing an open sheriff's seat in San Diego, and both of her victims held some political sway.

So I was on babysitting duty, a bullshit assignment that I was positive was punishment from my sergeant for reasons unknown. I had the highest rate of closed cases in the district, had received medals and was well-respected on our squad. Last year I'd closed a high-profile murder case that was in every L.A. newspaper.

But I'd also gotten drunk at our holiday party and flirted with the sergeant's wife, a sexy little submissive who liked me more than she wanted to admit.

Which is probably why I'd spent the last eight weeks of my life living in a car filled with fast food wrappers, operating on no sleep, and being slowly tortured by a man eater.

"I think she's just landed her next one, sir. I'm pretty positive of it."

I'd watched enough of her dinners to know. They almost always fucked her at the end of the night, that was a given, but it didn't necessarily go further than that.

Violet was careful. If something spooked her, she'd be gone in a flash. From what I could tell, they needed to be easily manipulated. They needed to become obsessed with her. They needed marriages that were crucial to their political career but a weakness for cheating.

"Who?" he asked.

I looked around, made sure no one could hear. "Jack Peterson. Venture capitalist in the Bay Area. Plus, his wife is the mayor's sister."

"Political aspirations?"

"That's the rumor," I said. "His uncle was a senator, and his brother has been sniffing around some county seats."

He was silent for a moment. "You need to close this case soon, Will."

We'd had this conversation once a week for the past three weeks.

"This is junior detective work. Watch her, catch her, bring her in. It shouldn't be taking you so long."

"There's no crime against sleeping with guys you meet at a bar. And that's all it looks like for now. I've got nothing." Which I'd convinced myself was true. "I need to stay on her for longer, sir."

From the corner of my eye, I watched Violet and Jack stand up and walk towards the door.

"I've got to go," I said crisply. "They're moving." I hung up before he could respond, a mistake I'd most likely pay for later. I watched Violet walk past tables, Jack's hand on the small of her back. I felt my palms itch. She usually taxied to the restaurant, which meant they'd be taking his car.

Mine was parked behind the valet station so I could follow them easily. I was so distracted watching her I didn't move fast enough when they stepped outside. I was closer to Violet than I'd ever been, just a few feet away. I busied myself on my phone, pretending to talk to a girlfriend.

"I know, sweetheart," I mumbled into the empty receiver. "I miss you too." I looked down and laughed softly, then said, "I'm on my way home. Can't you wait a little longer?"

I watched their feet, the way Jack kept moving closer and closer to her. She was like a bright star, drawing him closer, into her orbit. I knew the feeling.

I nodded, pretending to listen to my imaginary girlfriend, then hung up the phone. I glanced up to find Violet looking at me. It was only for a second, just a quick glance over her shoulder before sliding into the low body of Jack's car. Her bright blue eyes blazed right through me, and then she was gone. The door closed, and they pulled away.

I cursed, strode to my car, and prepared to tail them. My cock was hard and aching, had been the entire night. I cursed again—cursed those long legs and the sweet mystery between them, that hair I wanted to wrap around my fingers and yank, that throat I would mark with my teeth.

I cursed her entire game and tried to convince myself that I hated being twisted up in it.

I'd tailed Violet to dozens of mansions at this point. Jack Peterson lived in a modern one on the top of Telegraph Hill. It looked garish and slightly out of place. The lights of the bay twinkled in the background, and it was easy to imagine his life there, his sailboat on the weekends, martinis on the patio, the diamonds dripping from his wife's wrist.

I parked the car across the street and took out my binoculars. What I'd seen of this part of Violet's seduction was nothing more than fragments. It was always at night, and unless her suitor left the lights blazing, I couldn't spot her. Sometimes I'd catch them kissing at the front door or fooling around in the living room before heading elsewhere. On quiet nights, I found myself trying too hard to listen for the soft moans I knew she'd make.

I spent a lot of time wondering if she liked it. What she did in there.

What it felt like.

I shifted in my seat, reaching in the back for the bag of chips. My car now resembled (and smelled like) a college dorm room. Sometimes I nodded off and dreamt of Violet wearing my old college sweatshirt, sitting cross-legged on a bunk with a joint between her lips and a knowing smirk. I always woke up aroused and confused, only to find myself here, yet again, in front of some indistinct mansion.

Everything was starting to get to me.

A light on the second story switched on, and the curtains pulled back. I could see, so clearly, Jack and Violet. And so could anyone else if they happened to look out the window. It seemed risky for a man cheating on his wife. Had she convinced him to do it?

Through the binoculars, I watched Jack cup her cheek, tenderly. Her dark hair obscured her face as he dipped down to kiss her. I swallowed against another jolt of jealousy and mentally ran through the details of the case. I did this whenever I needed a distraction.

It almost never worked anymore.

He kissed her neck, and her head tilted back, face upturned towards the ceiling. I zoomed in as close as I could. Her blue eyes were open, staring. She looked... bored. Between them I sensed movement, and as I looked lower she was pulling his open belt through the loops, undoing his fly. Efficient.

Violet didn't seem to be about foreplay. Neither did Jack. He spun her around and pressed her against the big front window of his bedroom. My hands tightened on the binoculars.

He pulled her hair over her shoulder, licked up her throat. Again, she looked bored, shifting so she looked directly at me. Or, rather, directly out into the night since I was completely hidden in the darkness.

Jack undid the straps of her dress and pulled the top down to her waist, exposing the most beautiful breasts I had ever seen.

I shut my eyes against the sight, my cock pressing painfully against the fly of my jeans. I'd experienced this often when tailing suspects for weeks. I'd end up watching them so much that spying on their private business becomes second nature. And I'd be lying if I didn't admit I'd wanted this to happen, wanted to see Violet pressed, half-naked, against a window for my lazy perusal.

Now, in the moment, it felt wrong. I *knew* better. These nighttime stakeouts hadn't generated any leads, and it wasn't going to tonight. I needed another beer. I needed my motel bed. I needed to figure out what the fuck I was going to tell my boss tomorrow.

And that's when I caught something. A movement that didn't quite make sense.

I grabbed the binoculars and twisted until Jack and Violet were perfectly framed in the center of my view. He was fucking her—that was clear. The Dress was pulled up to her waist, and her thighs were as goddamn lickable as I imagined. I could see his face behind her, the tight grip of his hands, his steady thrusting. Those gorgeous, full breasts pushed against the windowpane. Her nipples were hard.

But it wasn't any of that that had caught my attention. Her eyes were staring right at me... not bored at all. I watched in a kind of daze as her right hand moved down her body, under her dress and into her panties. Her wrist started to move in tight, practiced circles.

And then she lifted up her left hand and waved at me.

2

WILL

Violet was masturbating for me, rubbing her nipples against the windowpane, her wrist moving quickly. Her eyes never left mine.

Violet knew that I was there. And she was *taunting* me. I tried to fight through the haze of lust and arousal to figure out how. To figure out why. To get one step ahead of her.

But instead, she pulled my strings from the second story of that mansion, and I obeyed.

I had my cock out in an instant and gripped it hard. I groaned at the contact. I knew, realistically speaking, she couldn't see me. But as soon as I started stroking, that smile broke across her face, and I almost came right there.

She rolled her nipple between her fingers, pinching, pulling, biting her lip as she did so. I groaned into my empty car, knew that if I had one last wish in this world it would be making Violet D'Allegra come just from licking her nipples. I'd done it once before. Had tied down my girlfriend at the time and sweetly tortured her for an hour before she came, shocked and happy, with her nipples in my mouth. With

Violet it wouldn't take that long; no, she wasn't that kind of woman. She'd come fast and hard, then beg me for another one.

Violet smiled at me again—dirty, knowing. With her left hand, she pulled her dress up farther, exposing the smooth skin of her belly and the delicious curve of her hips. Jack was either completely distracted or didn't care, still thrusting away, oblivious to everything she was doing.

Her hand was half obscured by her panties, which she slowly pulled to the side, giving me a better view. I could see the top of her pussy—shaved—and her index finger circling her clit quickly.

"Fuck," I growled, my hand moving just as fast. I needed to stop, to think. I needed to drive out of here as fast as possible. I needed to tongue-fuck her pussy deeper than she'd ever had before.

I needed to come. I watched Violet, wondering if I'd know when she did. Her mouth opened, and it looked like she'd let out something loud. On a hunch, I cracked the car door, listening.

There it was. The sounds of Violet's husky moans. You'd miss them if you didn't know they were there. I listened, watched a flush work its way across her chest, watched her face take on an almost pained expression. When her orgasm hit her, she half-collapsed across the window, Jack holding her up.

My orgasm was tight and fast and would have knocked me over if I wasn't sitting. I mimicked Violet, collapsing forward, my head on the steering wheel. I breathed deeply, trying to get my heart rate under control. I worried that the image of her coming while staring at me would be burned into my mind forever.

When I felt slightly normal, I looked up with the binoculars one last time. She was murmuring something to Jack, who had finished. She laughed a little, then turned back to me. Slowly, ever so fucking slowly, she raised her right index finger and sucked it into her mouth, tasting herself.

"Sweet Jesus Christ," I said. I drove away as fast as I could.

3

VIOLET

I watched Detective Will Furey drive away and smiled, contented.

"That was pretty good for you, huh, sweetheart?" Jack whispered into my ear, still behind me. He wasn't the worst I'd had, but he was still definitely not good. Not like I imagined Will would be.

"Mmmm," I half-moaned, and he laughed, leaving me. I turned around to see him walking into his bedroom. "When you make sounds like that, sweetheart, I get hard all over again."

I pulled the straps of my dress back up. More likely than not, that was the Viagra, but I held my tongue.

I took in Jack's master bedroom, which was easily twice the size of the trailer I'd grown up in. It was almost aggressively male and lacked any photos of family or friends. Or his wife. Her name was Sharon, and she did not look like me.

In my extensive research on Jack, I knew he owned two mansions in the area plus his summer home in Palm Springs and his winter home in North Lake Tahoe. He'd taken me to the house he kept for his mistresses. It was perfect. I smiled,

Cuffed

running my hands along the wall, searching for the best place to hide the tiny camera.

The sounds of water turned off, and Jack stepped back into the room. He was grinning like a fool and had the easy grace of a man who had never *not* been rich.

I'd "bumped into" Jack at a local happy hour spot I knew he frequented. I got a simple, slightly deluded pleasure knowing that Detective Furey spied on me as I spied on Jack. And Luke and Christopher and Gerald and Tim.

Jack, though, was turning out to be the winner.

I undid my straps again, letting my dress pool at my feet.

"*Fuck*," he said, running his hand over his mouth.

I walked slowly towards him, guessing correctly that the Viagra could let him go another round.

I slid my thumbs into the sides of my panties and lowered slowly.

"Jack, is this the house you bring your mistresses to?"

He nodded, watching the slow descent. "You're the first though," he said.

He thought I was a goddamned idiot. Good.

"That makes me happy," I purred, stepping closing to him, completely naked. Willingness to cheat? Check.

I stood an inch away from him. This close, I could see his pulse hammering at his throat. I made him nervous. There was nothing like knowing you made a man who was a fucking *billionaire* nervous.

Not too bad for trailer park trash.

I trailed my finger down his chest, his stomach, to his cock which was already hardening. I closed my eyes and groaned, imagining it was Detective Furey's.

Jack closed his fingers around mine. "You're amazing," he breathed.

"I don't have much experience," I said, slowly jerking his

cock. His eyes closed in pleasure. "But you bring something out in me, Jack. I've never felt this way before."

The lies got easier and easier the longer I did it. Easily manipulated? Check.

I dropped to my knees in front of him, still stroking. He hissed in a breath as he looked down at me. "You don't mind that I'm married?"

I shook my head, licking my lips. Sharon Peterson had been rich even before she married Jack. She came from a long line of wealthy men and politicians. Her brother was the mayor of San Francisco—beloved and much-admired. He brought her along all the time on the campaign trail. She had a natural charisma. Plus, she'd spent her life doing charity work. There were whispers she was vying to take his place once he termed out.

Jack, however, was being groomed for the State Senate. If all went to plan, they'd be racing each other towards political office.

Twice as many politicians in this marriage meant twice as easy to take down.

Jack wove his hands into my hair and pulled, not gently. I didn't have to pretend to like it. I looked up at him.

"And Violet... my wife can never, *ever* find out about this. Is that clear?"

A marriage too important to leave? Check.

I nodded and took the length of his cock into my mouth as deeply as I could. His grip tightened. I wondered what Will's cock would taste like.

That's what I'd been thinking about when I was touching myself. I couldn't see him in his car, not really, but I knew where he'd be. It was easy to spin out a quick and dirty fantasy. Me in the passenger seat of the car, penitent, contrite. Will's caught me but can't seem to turn me in. Can't seem to do anything except let his head fall back in gratitude when I undo his fly eagerly, taking out what I assumed would be a thick, veined cock. I wanted to hear the sound he'd make when it touched the back of my throat for the first time. I'd be balancing on my hands and knees, the gear shift brushing my stomach, his hand pulling my hair so tightly, tears coming to my eyes. And then I'd feel his fingers—three of them—pushing deep inside of me.

"Christ, Violet," Jack groaned loudly and then came in my mouth. I'd been so wrapped up in my fantasy, I hadn't noticed how close he was. But apparently I'd given a good performance. I hid my face, grimaced, then swallowed.

Jack tilted my chin up, cupping my cheek tenderly. "What are you doing to me?" he asked, amazed, his eyes searching mine.

Ability to become obsessed with me? *Check.*

4

VIOLET

I didn't stay the night, not the first time. You have to let them chase you.

"Call me later," I said breezily, stepping out in the night and into my waiting cab. He would. I'd ignore his call for the first day, then call him back on the second. And that's when I'd plant the camera.

I guessed I'd have to string Jack along for a few weeks, maybe a month. There was a point all men reached where they were essentially dumb with lust, and that's when I'd do it.

It was almost too simple. I'd come to their offices, a public place where they couldn't react too dangerously. I'd insert a USB drive into their computer and press play. Most people took a second to recognize themselves fucking on a screen. It'd take Jack a second; maybe he'd even think it was something kinky.

And then he'd know. Men like Jack didn't get through their lives without *someone* blackmailing them.

And mine was so, so typical.

"Here's the deal," I'd say calmly with the sounds of busy assistants and phones ringing in the background. "You will give me half a million dollars, in cash, or I will send this to your wife, the board of directors, and anyone else who gives a shit about you." Early on I found half a million dollars to be a sweet spot for extremely wealthy men. It was a lot to me, but it didn't sting them too bad (their pride was another issue).

The amount had weight to it, they had to take it seriously, but it wasn't enough to, say, kill me for it.

Although every time I had one of these meetings, I carried my little Derringer pistol tucked safely into my boot. I was a good shot. Had to be. But that was another story.

"I'm only going to ask you for this amount of money one time. That's my promise," I'd say, and I meant it. "Your promise is to not go to the police. I will, however, be keeping this on hand just in case you do."

I'd lean over, showing a generous amount of cleavage. It was funny how, even in the midst of a potentially career-ending situation, they always looked down my shirt.

"Do not test me on that," I'd say, and in that moment, I'd lift the mask. They'd see I was actually a little bit crazy. And not to be fucked with. Six hours later, cash in hand, I'd have my one bag packed, hailing a cab for the next city.

I made a mental note. It was probably time for me to change my name again. And my hair color. I was getting careless.

I also might have been enjoying myself a little too much.

Being a con artist was like riding a motorcycle down a dark highway without a helmet on. The tightening of my stomach on the curves, the breathlessness. My heart beating like a hummingbird's. The sharp, acrid fear that something bad would happen (which I was learning was its own kind of drug).

The thrill when it didn't.

I wondered from which parent I'd inherited this tilted

desire for recklessness and decided on my father. He didn't even stay long enough to see me born, just a few ultrasounds taped to the refrigerator. He rode in a motorcycle club, and it had been far too easy for him to blow through town, impregnate my mother, and blow on out—endlessly on the move, like a tumbleweed.

There was something inside of me that felt a similar tug, that craved to press my body against an open road and weep with relief.

My mother, however, taught me an entirely different lesson—that men thought with their dicks and were good for absolutely nothing. If I learned manipulation from anyone, it was her. The walls of the trailer we lived in were thin, especially since I slept on the couch-that-was-also-a-table, and she and her menagerie of lovers took the one bedroom.

They wouldn't stay long, but she had them twisted around her finger tight as a wedding ring.

When I was fifteen, I despised gym class and found that if I batted my eyelashes just right, my gym teacher would let me off. He had a wife too.

"Don't get married," my mother always said. "It complicates what it is—just sex." I knew that complication all too well. I *fed myself* off that complication.

I arrived back at the apartment I rented month-to-month in cash. I showered Jack away, slept fitfully for a few hours, Will in my dreams. The sound of my cell ringing woke me.

I glanced at it. It was Christopher.

"Good morning," I said, in a voice that was half-seduction, half-warning.

"I'm going to the police," he said, and my stomach dropped. He'd been sending me threatening text messages all week, and I'd ignored them.

Careless.

Cuffed

"I don't care if my wife finds out. I was going to divorce her anyway," he spit out. "You took my money. You held me *at gunpoint*. You need to pay."

Things with Christopher had gotten… complicated.

"How about we meet for coffee?" I said. I had a contingency plan I hadn't wanted to use but would if he forced me. "The Starbucks in Union Square in an hour?" Public, crowded, but I'd pack the pistol anyway.

"Bring the cash with you, or I'm calling the police," he said, then hung up.

I'd broken the rules on this one. I usually did one con per city, never staying for longer than it took me to score. After Christopher, though, I'd stayed in San Francisco, even knowing the risk it put me in. I'd first felt the burning gaze of Detective Will Furey on the back of my neck on a hot night in Los Angeles. Long before I ever saw Will's face, I felt his eyes on me and figured I was being tailed. At this point in my career, I'd conned five men, and I was sure at least one of them must have gone to the police.

I probably should have been more worried, but I couldn't seem to ever take it seriously. I hadn't met a man I couldn't easily manipulate.

And then I saw him, *really* saw him. I was in an outdoor cafe in L.A., waiting for a guy who'd end up going nowhere. Will was maybe ten tables away from me, hiding behind a newspaper like they do in the movies. I had my sunglasses on and was pretending to read on my phone—but I was waiting for him to reveal his face.

At some point, a waitress came over and asked for his order. The paper dropped and I immediately knew I was in trouble.

Detective Will Furey looked like the slightly fucked-up hero of my darkest fantasies. The kind I didn't like to admit to having. He gave her his order *like* an order, and I watched her grow flustered. He had dark eyes and dark hair that looked slightly shaggy and overgrown. I imagined threading my fingers into it and pulling. He was wearing the white button-up uniform of a detective, but his tie was undone, the first two buttons of his shirt open, exposing tan skin. His nose was strong, slightly crooked, and when he grinned at the waitress, she almost fainted.

Will *looked* nice, but I could tell it was a mask, veiling anger and frustration and maybe more. I saw how hard he worked to hide his ragged edges. I wondered what it would feel like to place my palm against the scruff of his three-day stubble. I wondered what it would feel like rubbing against the skin of my inner thighs.

I wondered if he would bite.

He'd tracked me up the coast to San Francisco, and I worried if I left he wouldn't follow. He was a problem, and it took me weeks to admit I liked it. I liked having his eyes on me. I liked knowing he watched. Last night, I had even liked taunting him.

It was one long, hot game of foreplay.

But I reminded myself every day that I needed to be smart—Will wasn't dumb, like the rest of them. I'd done my research. Detective Furey was decorated, high-achieving and well-respected. He played by the rules. He was a Good Guy. A good cop, even.

I showered, got ready, and wondered which outfit Will would like better. I pulled my hair up and back, packed the pistol in my purse and grabbed a cab to Union Square.

Christopher was a loose end—and now potentially a huge threat. I'd been distracted by Will during our entire relationship, so I didn't notice the warning signs I usually picked up on—like the fact that his marriage wasn't *that* important to him.

In the cab, I glanced in the rearview mirror and saw Will tailing me, a look of intense concentration on his face.

He was getting careless too.

When I arrived at the café, Christopher was waiting at a table for me outside already, which I didn't like. It gave him the upper hand. I hid my scowl, replaced it with a winning smile. I stalked over to him, hoping Will was watching my ass as I did so.

"Christopher," I said smoothly. "May I sit?"

The look he gave me could have killed. When I first met Christopher, he was the slightly shabby, incredibly stressed CEO of one of the biggest companies in San Francisco. He was easy to crack—I offered him relief in the form of mind-blowing sex.

Obsessed, manipulated... check, check.

He just didn't give a fuck about his wife. Unfortunately, during the four weeks I conned Christopher, I was secretly getting off on Will watching me, fighting conflicting urges to seduce him from afar and get the hell away from him as fast as possible.

As usual, my destructive side won, and when I walked into Christopher's office, file in hand, he took one look at me and said, "No fucking way."

The gun had been a mistake; I knew that now. I had never used it before, never wanted to. My game was control, not force. But I'd pulled it out of my purse and had it in his face so fast I surprised myself. I fucked up in a big way, though. Moments after I pulled the gun in his office, I glanced up into the blinking eye of a security camera.

Careless.

Again, I blamed Will for all of this. Especially since, on the day I had walked into Christopher's office, I'd caught Will, leaning against a wall a building down, pretending to make a call. I realized how tall he was, my eyes tracking down his lean torso. He looked... undone. In the elevator, I felt arousal curl low in my belly, thinking about undoing every part of Will Furey.

And then: gun, security camera, fuck-up.

That was what Christopher held over me and why I'd agreed to meet him.

"Where's the fucking money?" he asked, and I sat primly in response.

"I don't have your money, Christopher." I said, leaning back and crossing my legs. I'd worn a terribly short skirt, guessing that was Will's favorite. I couldn't see Will but felt him behind me.

"And why the fuck not?" His eyes were bloodshot, and he was gripping his coffee mug like his life depended on it.

"Because you gave me that money, sweetheart. You know..." I leaned forward, lowered my voice. "For all of the dirty, vile sex acts you made me perform."

His face reddened. "You seemed to enjoy yourself." I never did, but I was a great actress.

"Plus," I continued, moving in for the kill. "You have some big life changes coming your way. Isn't that right... Dad?"

I watched the surprise move over Christopher's face. "What are you talking about?"

"I'm talking about the fact that your wife is currently twelve weeks pregnant. And for four of those, you were fucking *me*—the first four, actually. If you go to the police and your wife finds out your mistress has blackmailed you, she'll rake you over the coals in your divorce settlement. And when she shows some judge the evidence that during the earliest parts of her *pregnancy*, instead of taking care of her and your unborn child, you were fucking someone?" I leaned forward for effect. "Say goodbye to custody."

Christopher had desperately wanted children. He'd shared that with me during those quiet moments after sex when every man unloads his deepest desires. It helps that I'm their beautiful mistress—they want to impress me too.

It also helps to do your research.

"You wouldn't," he said, face pale.

I laughed. "You know me better than that, Christopher." I stood, towering over him. "Go to the police and watch the rest of your life fall apart."

I turned on unsteady legs and strode away. I heard Christopher half-yell, "Fuck you, bitch," but I'd heard much, much worse in my life. We trailer trash usually have.

My heart was pounding, and I hoped like hell the plan had worked. I didn't want to ever see Christopher again, and I sure as shit didn't plan on going to jail because of one mistake.

My phone vibrated in my purse, and I checked it. It was Jack. Right on schedule. I smiled, considered answering it, and that's when a pair of strong hands grabbed me around the arm and dragged me into the alley.

My back was against a wall in an instant. I opened my mouth to scream, but a hand clamped down on it. I hated to admit to myself all these years that this was my darkest fear—to be killed in an alley by an angry mark.

"Open your eyes, Violet," a voice said, rough and deep. And that's when I knew who it was.

I obeyed, taking in his features up close. Will let go of my mouth.

"Detective Furey, I presume?" He placed his hands on either side of my head, boxing me in with his body. His face was less than a foot from my own. His dark gaze was so intense I felt completely naked. Devoured.

Then, I remembered that I had the power.

"So you know who I am," he growled.

"I do," I replied casually. "I know you've been tailing me for some time now. Enjoying yourself?" I asked with an arched eyebrow.

His full lips tugged up into a snarl. "Enjoying watching you destroy men's lives? No, I'm not."

"I doubt you've seen me actually destroy anyone's life," I said, all innocence. "But you *have* seen me fuck, haven't you?" I bit my lip, watching the arousal heat in his eyes. Point for me.

He looked at me like he was examining a new species. "You're not afraid of me at all?"

"What's to be afraid of?"

He stared until I felt myself flush. "I know Christopher Doggett is one of your victims. But I've never seen you go back after the take. What does he have on you, Violet?"

I widened my eyes in disbelief. "Oh, I'm sorry. I didn't realize I was being questioned, Detective Furey? Would you like to take me down to the precinct?"

I reached forward and ran my finger down the middle of his chest, trying to ignore how hard it was. I looked up at him from underneath my lashes. "And I'm pretty sure I have the right to a lawyer."

His hand shot out and grabbed my finger, stopping its slow descent. He grabbed my other hand and pulled both of them down to my sides, holding them there and bringing us two inches closer.

My breath caught in my chest, and he noticed it, grinning slightly. *Arrogant prick*, I thought.

He lowered his mouth until it was right against my ear. Every nerve ending in my body lit up like a Christmas tree. His breath was warm and steady, and I fought not to lean into his touch.

"I'm pretty sure, *Violet,* that you're getting sloppy," he murmured, lips almost touching the edges of my ear. He moved his mouth to under my ear, my jaw. "And I'm pretty sure that Christopher has something on you that's making you nervous." I felt his breath trace down my neck, and I shamelessly tilted my head, allowing him greater access.

I would have given every cent of Christopher's money to feel his lips.

Will threaded his fingers through mine, pushing them against the wall until it hurt. His breath moved down my neck. "And I know I've got two guys with my Sergeant right now willing to testify that you blackmailed them."

My stomach clenched. He had to be lying.

His mouth moved back to my ear again, teasing it. I almost wept. "And I know I've been watching you for a long time."

"You sound angry about that, Detective," I said, breathlessly.

He paused, and then scraped his teeth down my earlobe. I let out a sharp moan, and his hand clamped over my mouth, silencing it.

His face was an inch away. "I'm not angry, Violet. I just know your game now. I know it *very* well. And I'm not going to fall for it." He let his hand drop and grabbed my unbound hand again. I couldn't stop staring at his mouth.

"Looks like you already have," I said.

He responded by yanking my hands up to the side of my head, pinning me. I was more aroused than I'd ever been in my life, and he'd barely touched me. We were both breathing heavily, his lips hovering over mine.

I wouldn't do it. I couldn't do it.

I did. I closed the gap and pressed my lips against his, kissing him for all I was worth. He groaned, taking me with his mouth. That was the only way to describe it. I was utterly and completely taken over by Will Furey. He kissed me roughly, like a drowning man coming up for air. He kissed me like he'd fuck me—hard and thorough. I kept trying to angle my body into his, my pussy desperate for contact, but he wouldn't let me.

His tongue teased against mine, over and over, driving me half-mad with desire. I wanted to climb the wall. I wanted to drop before him on my knees and beg for his cock. I wanted to know what else his tongue could do.

So I bit it, kind of hard. He swore, pulling back, touching his finger to his tongue. I'd drawn blood. I thought he'd be mad, but the look he gave me promised a different kind of punishment.

He released me, stepping back. With one hand he grabbed my chin, tilting until I looked up at him.

"And what game are you falling for, Violet?"

His gaze burned right through me. And then he turned around and left.

5

WILL

Violet was a hunter. Yet she'd trembled when I touched her. Flushed skin, heavy breathing, eyes half-lidded and dreamy. I didn't really think she'd kiss me, but when she did, it was hungry and hard, and I knew, if I let her, she'd pull me right under.

Two minutes longer, and I would have given her what she wanted. I held back, though, wanting to wrench back a little bit of the power she'd taken from me.

I'd gotten under her skin. The knowledge gave me a sick satisfaction I wasn't proud of. After the alley, I drove back to my motel and stood under the shower for a long, long time, aching for release, the scent of her skin on my hands.

I'd been a detective for ten years. I was a Good Cop. I followed every rule, expected those who worked for me to be ethical, smart. Honest.

And I worked so fucking hard to hide my darkest instincts. During my ten years on the force, I'd behaved. Even when witnesses threw themselves at me, when new widows begged me to fuck them, when the girlfriends of my squad-mates showed up at my door, half-naked and half-drunk, I always behaved. Cops had power, a lot of it. Fuck, I craved that. But I took those desires elsewhere, *away* from the job.

Clubs, strangers from the internet. Short-term girlfriends who liked their coffee with a bit of kink and a lot of submission. Women who could handle a sexual appetite that sometimes shamed me.

Eight weeks of Violet, and the only thing I wanted to do with my power was abuse it. I broke basically every rule in the fifteen minutes I was in that alley with her. I wished I had broken more. Shit, she could report me and have me thrown from the force, have me stripped of the badge I'd worn proudly for a decade... for kissing.

When the sergeant first pulled me in, he showed me a picture of her, and I was already a goner. That night I'd gone out and fucked a stranger in the bathroom at a bar, overcome with a wild lust that started low in my gut and made me plunge my cock into her over and over again.

The men we interviewed described her as a temptress, a skilled puppeteer. The word "evil" was also bandied about, and even though I didn't know her, I shut that shit down fast. Some part of me, deep inside, respected this wild con artist. She was a thing of beauty. I wanted her even then—to be tempted by her. To be played.

At the restaurant, now, I sat close to Jack and Violet, close enough that I could see her agitation. It didn't matter anymore that I was watching her. She knew. And she was unsettled.

She usually waited more than one day to let her marks take her out again, but she must have accepted Jack's desperate offer. And you could see how desperate he was. Hands all over her, constantly—on her thighs, her arms, brushing through her hair. I almost tore the menu in half.

He was already obsessed.

She was wearing her favorite spike heels, a red mini-skirt,

and a black top that clung to her breasts. Her lipstick was a dark red, darker than blood, and she looked lethal.

She had her armor on tonight. But she was only half-there.

Her smiles were tight. A few times I overhead Jack make a joke, and she'd laugh but two beats too late. She drummed her fingers on the seat of her chair, twisting that gold ring.

I sipped my beer and watched. Waited.

A text came through from the sergeant.

Another possible victim just came forward. Same story, same name, same description. He's at the precinct now and says he's got something big. I'll call you after the interview.

A few seconds went by and then: *Try to bring her in tonight if you can.*

I looked up, and Violet was staring at me, her blue eyes flashing. I nodded, raised my beer in a toast. She covertly flipped me the middle finger under the table.

I grinned, feeling slightly unhinged. Then, I turned my cell phone off.

Jack looked relaxed and comfortable throughout the entire dinner—like a rich man with a new mistress willing to do every filthy thing he'd ever fantasized about. He looked like prey.

Run, I wanted to tell him.

I kept my eye out for Christopher since he'd seemed a little psycho at the coffee shop. I wondered briefly if that was the possible victim, and my stomach knotted.

I wanted to arrest Violet. *I wanted to arrest Violet.* I repeated this phrase like a mantra as Violet traced her fingers down Jack's arm, bringing his fingers to her mouth for a kiss. She sucked his index finger into her mouth, her lips leaving a stain of red.

I shifted uncomfortably in my chair, remembering the sound of her moaning against my hand.

A few minutes later, Jack stood to go to the bathroom. "I know, I know," I heard him say, pressing the palm of his hand against her face. "I'll be gone for just a minute, sweetheart." I fought an eye-roll. Even distracted, Violet had him trussed up and tied to the railroad tracks.

She was also furious with me. It rolled off her in waves, and as soon as Jack was out of sight, she turned, ever-so-subtly, until she was facing me. Her eyes met mine, legs uncrossing. I shrugged at her and leaned back in my chair.

Those blue eyes narrowed, and then she tracked her fingers up her toned thighs and to the edge of her skirt. My jaw clenched.

She smiled wickedly, fingers pulling at her skirt, lifting it higher, slow centimeter by slow centimeter. I'd never wanted to see anything more in my life than Violet's pussy, bare and exposed. I thought about that as I held her gaze, not breaking it. She lifted even higher, and I held it, trapped her with it. Pinned her like a goddamn insect under a microscope.

Violet D'Allegra blushed and looked away. I arched my eyebrow—I'd won. Over her shoulder I saw Jack walking towards her. I caught her eye and cleared my throat.

She took my cue, and my skin burned with our brief moment of complicity. The mask dropped down. She closed her legs and arranged herself for Jack.

It was going to be a very long night.

6

WILL

*V*iolet had taken Jack to a club, and he'd been eager, probably hoping to reclaim one last vestige of his youth with his hot, young mistress. I followed them from the restaurant, walking a hundred feet behind. I kept my eyes off the sway of her ass, instead mentally compiling the evidence I had to arrest Violet on the spot.

It wasn't much. But it was enough—had been enough for weeks now. Ten years of my life dangled over an open drain.

The music was loud, and the lighting was bad—she'd done that on purpose so I couldn't hear what they were saying. On the second date, Violet laid a lot of groundwork, sharing some sob story, building trust, probably giving them a half-hand-job on the cab ride home.

She was doing the same tonight, pulling a rhythm-less Jack onto the dance floor. It was small and crowded. Leaning against the bar, I was only fifteen feet away from them.

Violet ground her ass against Jack, lacing her hands over her head and around his neck, baring the entire length of her body for me. I swallowed against my irritation. This was payback for the restaurant, for not falling under her spell.

She gyrated her hips, her eyes watching me dangerously. I glanced at my watch and looked away, catching the eye of a sexy redhead down the bar. I winked at her. She winked back. I glanced back at Violet, and she gave me a sardonic smirk. I fought back a smile, taking a sip of my drink instead.

I tried to distract myself with whatever was on the TV over the bar. Moments later, I felt movement behind my shoulder. I turned and was suddenly face-to-face with Violet.

"Excuse me," she purred. "Can my boyfriend and I squeeze in here?" Jack was nuzzling her neck, oblivious.

"Of course," I rasped, sliding down to make room. There was barely enough space for them, so Violet lodged herself against my side, ass against my hip.

I heard her say, "Let's order drinks," to Jack, and then she was kissing him, her hand on his chest.

I turned back to the TV, hell-bent on ignoring her, when I felt her hand settle on my cock. I'd been hard since the restaurant, and she squeezed me between her fingers.

If I hadn't been holding onto the bar, I would have fallen over. She kissed Jack passionately and palmed me through my jeans, unleashing weeks of pent-up tension. Almost against my will, I turned slowly until she had better access, my eyes watching her hand. If Jack hadn't been there, I would have undone my fly and let her jerk me off in front of everyone.

Glancing at Jack, making sure his eyes were truly closed, I traced my fingers up the back of Violet's legs and under her skirt, my thumb caressing the swell of her ass. She gripped my cock, hard, letting me know how she felt about that. I looked around to see if anyone noticed. They didn't. I traced small circles on the backs of her thighs, stroking the sensitive skin. She pushed her palm down harder, and my eyes closed in pleasure. Without the over-stimulation of the strobe lights and bass and endless bodies, I could focus. It was just her hand and my hand, stroking, teasing, seeking.

"You guys want a drink?"

All three of us turned, startled, to face the bartender who was now yelling at us. Violet laughed nervously, and Jack said, "Two vodka sodas, please."

He immediately went back to kissing her. Violet had let go of me in surprise, but I kept my hand where it was. My thumb slid to the edge of her panties, teasing the sides. She was soaked through.

And then, just as suddenly, she was pushing Jack away, drinks forgotten, and throwing me a look that just about knocked me down.

Try to bring her in if you can.

Try to bring her in.

Try to.

Minutes later, when Jack left for the bathroom, I stalked over and grabbed her before she could turn around. I grasped her waist and pulled her tight against me.

She turned her head, mouth against my ear, and circled her hips once, twice. "Detective Furey," she breathed. "Is that a roll of a quarters or—"

I gripped her harder, stopping her movements. "Tell Jack you're sick and you need to leave."

She started to laugh, but I cut her off. "Leave him this instant, or I swear to fucking God I will arrest you on this dance floor in front of all of these people, in front of Jack. You're coming with me. I'll be waiting for you two blocks up."

I let go of her, and she spun around, disbelief and anger clashing on her beautiful face.

"If you're not there in ten minutes, you'll be leaving here in a squad car. And not mine."

I turned and left before I could change my mind. I pushed

through the sea of bodies until I finally made it outside. I walked quickly towards our meeting point, checking my watch. I didn't have a fucking clue what I'd do if she didn't show.

I didn't have a fucking clue what I'd do if she did show.

And I didn't have to wait for long. I heard the sharp click of those heels behind me almost immediately. I turned around to face an extremely furious Violet.

"Evening," I said smoothly. I reached behind me and unhooked my handcuffs. She saw them, and she stopped walking.

I grabbed her arm tightly and yanked until she started again.

"*Fuck* you, Will," she spat. "Since when is it a crime in this city to have dinner with someone?"

I reached for her wrist and hooked the first cuff around it. Fear flashed over her eyes briefly before she hid it.

"It's a crime when you blackmail them for money, gorgeous," I replied, snapping the cuff on. "And I should begin by saying that Violet D'Allegra, you have the right to remain silent. Anything you say can and will be used against—"

"Like the fact that a detective has been stalking me for weeks now? Watching me undress? Is that in your Police Academy training?"

I stopped in front of my car and pushed her against the door. Her eyes blazed. "Do you try to seduce every cop that tries to stop you? Or just the ones you *want* to fuck?" I asked quietly.

"Please," she laughed, although it was strained. "You're all the same."

I shoved my thigh between her legs, spreading her. I brought my lips within an inch of hers and held them there. We stood, locked like that, until she whimpered.

What the hell was I doing?

I took a step back, reaching over her to open the door to the backseat. "Get in," I said. She did, looking dignified, like she was doing me a favor. I slammed the door behind her, leaning against it, my eyes closed.

Just get her downtown. Any other cop would have brought her in for questioning weeks ago.

I got behind the wheel, my heart pounding. In the rearview mirror, Violet tilted her chin at me defiantly. But she looked terrified.

My chest ached. I turned around. I shouldn't have. Maybe if I hadn't—maybe if I'd kept my eyes straight ahead, none of it would have happened.

But I did. And the sight of Violet with her legs spread, skirt high, and her hands cuffed behind her back was too much for me. My darkest desires reared up, unashamed and greedy. My future as a police officer narrowed to a sharp point, but Violet blazed white hot.

I didn't want to be good anymore.

7

WILL

I climbed into the backseat and crouched before her legs, like every single filthy fantasy I had. Her expression was mixed—a bit of surprise and that damn defiance.

In the course of the evening, her hair had come slightly undone, and I reached forward, brushing a lock behind her ear.

I gently massaged the muscles of her neck, which had tightened in apprehension. She closed her eyes, sighing softly.

"Violet." I said, and it felt like a question. She leaned into my hand but kept her eyes closed.

I threaded my fingers through her hair, pulling gently.

"Violet," I said, harsher this time. Her eyes opened, and she gave me her answer. A nod. A *please.* "Yes," she whispered. "Yes, you can."

In total reverence, I cupped her breasts, her nipples already hardening against the palms of my hands. I hissed in a breath.

She half-shot off the car seat.

Cuffed

"Shhhh," I said softly, circling her nipples with my thumbs. She bit her lip, eyes wide. "Violet, I need you to tell me something."

I twisted, lightly, and a groan escaped her mouth. I grinned at her. "Violet?"

"Yes?" she gasped, and I rewarded her by leaning forward and sucking her nipple through the fabric. She cried out.

I moved to her legs, open in front of me. I pushed them wide, as wide as they could go, and settled between them. I grabbed her skirt and shoved it up over her hips. She wore the world's smallest black panties. I cursed at the sight of them.

Violet was watching me in total fascination. "What's your question, Will?" she asked breathlessly. I pinched the skin of her thigh, and she yelped. "Patience," I said.

With my thumb I pulled back the material, exposing her shaved pussy to my eager eyes.

"Christ, Violet," I groaned. She was soaking wet.

I placed my thumb on her clit, circling gently. Her hips shot forward.

"When..." I began, running my tongue from her knee to her inner thigh, "was the last time..." I continued, biting the smooth skin, "someone gave you pleasure?"

I blew a soft, hot breath on her clit. She groaned in frustration.

"I won't give it to you if you won't talk to me, Violet. I like talking."

She glared at me, a lock of hair in her face. I brushed it aside, and she caught my finger between her teeth. I arched an eyebrow. She released it.

"A really... a really long time," she finally said, looking away. I cupped her face, turning her to look at me.

"Do you trust me?"

She searched my face for a moment and then nodded. To this day, I don't know why. But she did. And I trusted her, in all her twisted glory. I cupped her face in my hands and kissed her, groaning at the contact. For a moment, that was all we needed, and I fell, gladly, into the sensation of her lips against mine, of the tiny, hungry sounds she made.

Then I slid my finger deep inside of her. She was tight and wet and hot as fuck. Her head fell back against the seat, and she shifted her hips for me. I slid deeper.

"Good girl," I murmured against her ear. I kissed every inch of her neck, and she moaned. I remembered the night at Jack's mansion, hearing just the hint of her in the night. This was better.

I could feel her G-spot against the pad of my finger. I circled it softly as I sucked her nipple into my mouth again.

"Oh, go fuck yourself, Will," Violet said, in a half moan-half sigh. I chuckled against her skin.

"I will do no such thing," I said, gazing up at her. I added a second finger, and she cursed again.

It was almost too much to hope for with Violet. I didn't always find someone who met *all* of my needs. But beyond the anger and fear and irritation I saw in her eyes as I cuffed her, I also sensed arousal.

I finger-fucked her slowly and watched her reactions, mesmerized. She was goddamn beautiful.

"You like being cuffed," I told her.

"I don't," she said, but a half-smile tugged at her lips. I twisted my fingers, and her head fell back again.

"You do. You want to submit to me."

She shook her head in agony. She was lying. I slid my thumb over her clit, and she almost lost it. Then I leaned down and replaced my thumb with my tongue.

Cuffed

"Oh my *God*," she moaned. She tasted musky and sweet. She tasted perfect. I licked her steadily for a minute, completely indulging myself. I might not have Violet cuffed and acquiescent ever again.

Then I pulled back.

"What the—" she groaned. She clenched around my fingers.

"Violet. Do you want me to make you come?" She nodded, biting her lip. I reached forward and pinched her nipple, hard. "What did I say about talking?"

She tilted her chin at me, and I couldn't help but smile at her. She was being a brat, but I felt her yielding. Could make her yield, if I wanted to.

I fucked her quickly, sliding a third finger inside, stretching her. "*Please*," she begged, almost incoherently. "Please, please *please*..." she moaned, over and over again.

It was what I needed. I bent my head and lapped at her clit. With a growl I grabbed her hips, pulling her off the seat and closer to my mouth. I could look up and watch as I ravished her pussy, her earthy smell in my mouth, my fingers sliding in and out, her cries of pleasure.

She liked it when I circled my tongue in hard, tight circles, so I went as slowly and gently as possible. Her ragged groans of frustration only spurred me on, and I was positive I was about to become the first man to orgasm without being touched. Violet was flushed and half out of her mind. It was intoxicating.

She was already close, and I wanted to give in so badly. I stroked over her G-spot and sucked her clit into my mouth. The words tumbling out of her mouth weren't English but something along the lines of "Yes, yes, *fuck Will, yes*" over and over.

And so I stopped.

Violet's eyes opened, confused and furious. She was out of breath and panting.

"Wha... what," she mumbled, staring at me. I sat up, pushed her legs together, and wiped my mouth with a grin.

"No no," she said, leaning forward, trying to spread her legs. I held them tight as a vise. "Why did you stop? Why did you..."

I shook my head, cradling the side of her face with my palm. She half-sobbed, a tear sliding down her cheek. I don't even think she knew she was crying.

It had been a long night for Violet.

"I've got you, gorgeous. I've got you," I said softly, tracing my thumb over her cheekbone. "But this is your punishment."

Her eyes narrowed. I thought she might spit on me. I brought my face an inch from hers, hovering my lips over her mouth. I needed her to understand.

"You've spent the last eight weeks torturing me like no woman *ever* has before. You had me so twisted up—*fuck* Violet. Do you have any idea what that feels like? To want something so badly but know you can't have it?" Our eyes met, and she nodded, slowly. I held my breath.

"Take me, Will," she finally said, on a long sigh. "Please just... take me somewhere. *Please*."

Whatever path I thought we'd go down this night, I couldn't stop it now. It was dark, and I wanted it.

"Do you still trust me?"

"Yes."

"You're going to sit in this backseat on the edge of orgasm for the entire time it takes me to drive to my motel."

A pause. "*Yes.*"

"Yes what?" I wanted to play.

The look she gave me spoke volumes. "Yes... sir."

I hated to stop touching her, but I did, sliding back over and into the front seat. My hands shook when I placed them on the steering wheel.

I looked in the rearview mirror and met her gaze. "Let's go, then."

8

VIOLET

*D*etective Will Furey was a sick bastard.

I wanted him more than anything I'd ever wanted. I *did* like being cuffed. Not that I'd ever admit that to him.

Whatever fear I'd felt at my potential future in prison had faded to a sharp knifepoint of desire. Every cell in my body throbbed. One more second... *one more second*, and I would have had the best orgasm of my life. He was as skilled and sexy as I imagined. More, actually. And, in a decision I'd probably regret later, I'd begged him to take me.

The car ride to the motel was short and tense. A dull ache had settled between my shoulders where they were pushed together by the handcuffs. A slick wetness coated the inside of my thighs. My nipples throbbed. And all I could do was stare at the back of Will's head and wonder what he was going to do to me.

I wasn't lying when Will wrenched my secret from me—I hadn't been pleasured in a long time. I had sex for money, basically. I was an escort whose clients didn't know it. I faked orgasms like a porn star. Part of the decision I'd made to become a con artist also involved saying goodbye to sex—*good* sex—at least for the time being.

And Will... well, he brought out something in me I thought no man ever would. "Never let them see you weak," my mother had always said, and now I was cuffed in the backseat of a cop car moments away from pleading.

Never *ever* did I want it this way.

Except as soon as I saw Will, part of me knew, knew that we were traveling down the same road together. Knew that I could submit to him in the way my body had not-so-secretly craved.

Knew that, in yielding, I really held the power.

His hands on the steering wheel were strong, his forearms toned. I'd felt his barely restrained strength as he kneeled at my feet—the way he'd held my legs open, his clever tongue, the vibrations against my clit as he groaned over and over. The wilder I got, the more he fought for control.

Goddammit. My head lolled back, the memories lighting every nerve ending on fire. I rolled my hips against the seat, trying to find a friction. I was so close.

"Violet." Just my name in his stern, hoarse voice. A warning.

"What?" I breathed. He liked when I talked back.

"Do you want my cock inside you?"

I moaned, almost painfully turned on. "Yes," I whispered.

"Then don't come."

I stopped.

He turned two more times and then pulled into a parking lot. It was such a seedy motel—bright pink sign, the "Vacancy" letters flickering on and off. In the back I could see a murky-looking pool, a few chairs scattered around it. I swallowed nervously. We were here.

He opened the car door, grabbed the backs of my wrists

and hauled me up and out. I looked around, scared someone would see, but we were the only people in the parking lot.

His hands were shaking.

Will had me inside his motel and up against the door in no time. He kissed me passionately, and I tasted myself.

I wasn't expecting it. I leaned desperately into his touch, loving the feel of his lips on mine. He pressed his big, solid body against me. I wantonly spread my legs, and I felt the bulge of his jeans line up right where I needed it. He didn't move, though, and I found myself trying to climb him. Which, I was learning, was not easy when your hands were cuffed behind your back.

He pulled away with a crooked grin. And then he spun me around and pushed my face against the doorframe. I couldn't see at all. I liked it.

Will's lips landed against my ear. "You can't have it yet."

I leaned my head back against his shoulder, loving the feeling of his mouth moving against my neck, kissing, licking. Then he bit me, hard. And again, so hard he'd be leaving marks.

Possessive son-of-a-bitch.

His hands moved down my back and to the handcuffs. I heard the jingle of keys and then a tugging sensation against my wrists. With a click, they were free. I didn't want to move them just yet, but Will did, allowing the blood to flow. I hissed a little, and he brought my right wrist to his mouth. He kissed the sensitive skin over my pulse, massaging. He did the same for the other one.

"Put your hands against the wall." I did. He massaged the aching muscles of my shoulders with his skilled fingers, almost in apology. His tenderness had me wary.

He reached around me, cupping my breasts. I arched into

him, moaning. And then he ripped my shirt completely in half.

That was more like Will.

"I liked that shirt," I said. He responded by yanking up my skirt and spanking my bare ass.

I gasped, the shock of the sting reverberating throughout my entire body.

"I didn't ask if you liked it," he replied calmly. He unzipped the skirt and yanked it roughly down my legs. My panties went the way of my shirt, ripped in half and tossed to the side.

I was suddenly and completely naked in front of a man who'd tried to arrest me not an hour earlier.

"You're keeping those heels on."

Well, almost naked. And still on the edge of orgasm.

I smiled against the door, feeling his eyes all over me. I heard the sound of a chair being moved.

"Will?" I asked, slightly turning. He was sitting in it, one leg crossed over the other. Staring.

"I could do this all night, Violet."

I trembled, feeling his eyes between my legs. It was almost as if he was touching me.

"What?"

"Stare at your perfect body. Listen to you beg. Watch you get wetter and wetter." His voice grew even more hoarse. "I want to watch it drip out of you, gorgeous."

I squirmed against the door. I didn't want to beg again, wanting to distance myself from the wanton creature I'd become in the car.

"Bend over for me," he said softly. I did, sliding my hands down the door until I could grip the doorknob. My ass hovered about a foot from Will's face. I could feel his breath.

"Beautiful." Both of his hands teased over my skin, sometimes massaging, sometimes lightly scratching. It was soothing and arousing all at the same time.

I felt his mouth hovering, and he ran his tongue from the back of my thigh and up and over my ass. I shivered when he bit me.

"I'm going to ask you about trust one more time," he said. "I want to do things to you, Violet. But you need to use a safe word with me. I want you to feel safe, gorgeous."

"O–okay,"

"Tell me what it is."

His hand massaged my ass, waiting. Soothing.

"Handcuffs," I finally said. Will kissed the small of my back.

"Perfect," he rasped. Then his hand delivered a ringing slap to my ass. My hands tightened on the doorknob.

"I want to do things just like that."

His hand rubbed over where he'd spanked me, setting off another round of sparks in my body. I moaned and leaned into his touch. He laughed darkly. I'd never really wanted it before, with other lovers, but Will was uncovering fantasies I'd never admitted to anyone.

"I want that," I finally said, and he spanked me again.

Pain shot through me, twisted with an intense pleasure. He was good at it. I groaned loudly as he spanked me a third time, and I almost fell over.

I felt his arms strong, like a vice, clutch my hips. "I've got you," he said again and rubbed harshly over my skin. "Your ass is so pretty and pink for me now."

I heard the chair scoot closer and his hands grip my ass cheeks, spreading me. He blew a long, hot breath over my quivering skin. "Your pussy is so pink and pretty for me too." He groaned and then plunged his tongue inside me.

I cried out, almost coming at the contact, but he wouldn't

let me do that. Instead, his tongue tormented me, licking deep inside, over and over. The louder I moaned, the more his hands shook with the effort of holding back.

It felt so goddamn good. And then he spanked me again. This one hurt, stung really, and I bit back a curse. "I didn't tell you to come, remember?" He spanked me again and again, the sounds of skin against skin and my cries filling the room.

He dipped his thumb inside me, coating it with my arousal. He moved his thumb to my asshole, circling it, testing. I'd never done that before, but at this point I would have let him do absolutely anything to me. He pushed, just a little, and then went back to teasing. I groaned in frustration.

"Dirty girl," he said appreciatively. "We might get to that tomorrow, but tonight all I want is this."

He pushed two fingers inside me roughly, spanking me at the same time. I was half out of my mind, strung tight as a bow. I thought it would never end, and then he stopped, grabbed me by the hair, and yanked me up against his hard body.

"Please," I sobbed, all concerns for being too wanton and desperate flying out the window.

"You're not ready," he growled against my ear. My legs were spread and open, but only the cool air of the motel room licked between them. I wanted contact. I wanted relief. I wanted to come.

Instead, Will sat down and pulled me across his lap, spreading my legs wider but not touching. His fingers traced over my breasts, and I sighed. With precision, he rolled my nipples between his fingers and pleasure shot straight to my core. He pushed me back until my head was cradled against his shoulder and I could watch everything he did. I hadn't been able to see his face and he'd become... animalistic. Starved-looking. I was the only thing in the world for him.

It was addictive.

He kept rolling and pinching my nipples, and I spread my legs wider, my clit desperate for attention. He smiled at me, reading my thoughts.

"You're so perfect like this, Violet. I wish I could keep you on the edge forever."

"Don't you fucking *dare*," I moaned as he pinched my left nipple. He chuckled softly, then dipped his head and took my breast into his mouth.

He licked and sucked and bit for what felt like hours but was probably only minutes. He only stopped to stare at me once and said, "You know, the first night you met Jack, I fantasized about this."

I was barely human at that point, my voice ragged from the sounds being wrenched from my throat. "What?" I asked, my hand drifting down to touch my clit. If I could *just...*

He grabbed it, halting my progress.

"I fantasized about licking your nipples until you came."

"*Fuck*," I moaned, head tilting back.

"But I think I want to do something else." He lifted me up, since I couldn't stand at that point, and hauled me onto my hands and knees on the bed. I heard the sounds of clothes coming off, of his belt sliding through loops, and I tried to turn around.

"Eyes forward."

I complied but wanted to see his body so badly. I'd thought almost exclusively about what Will's cock looked like for weeks.

Soft leather traced over the backs of my legs. His belt. My heart thudded. And then he hit me with it.

It stung, worse than his hand, and I liked it so fucking much. He did it again, and I moaned. I dropped my face into the bed, arching higher into the belt as it stung the skin of my ass again.

Will slid his hand down my naked spine and threaded his fingers into my hair.

"God*dammit* Violet," he said, and I smiled, pleased. Again and again, he spanked me, only this time his groans were louder than mine. I couldn't see, but I imagined him standing there, tall and magnificent with his hard cock.

I turned and peeked through my hair. My breath caught. I was right, and he was more beautiful than I imagined. Strong thighs and a narrow waist, a defined chest and broad shoulders. The muscles of his arm bunched as he wielded his belt.

His cock stood straight out of his body, hard and wet with pre-cum. My mouth watered.

Just as suddenly he stopped, and I worried he'd caught me staring. Instead, he crawled onto the bed behind me and gripped my hips, pulling me back against him. The feel of his cock brushing against my pussy was the most divine sensation I'd ever felt. And then I felt his fingers move to my clit, rubbing in small circles.

After the car and the spanking and the tongue-fucking and the nipple play and then *more* spanking, I was seconds from coming. He stopped again, and I almost gave up completely, but it was just to grab a condom. I heard the sounds of the packaging tearing. It was the most erotic sound I'd ever heard.

He went back to rubbing my clit, and my body tensed, waves of pleasure climbing higher and higher. And then he slid easily inside of me, and everything crashed.

I screamed, coming hard and sharp and stronger than I ever had before. He kept his finger on my clit and fucked me in fast, shallow strokes, prolonging it. I almost tore the bed sheet in half. My orgasm lingered, tiny sparks of heat as Will slowed his strokes, dragging every inch of his cock over my too-sensitive nerves and rubbing tiny circles over my clit.

The waves built again so quickly I wasn't ready for it. It was too much sensation. My second orgasm surprised me, stealing my breath. His arm snaked around my shoulders, and he lifted me up and onto his lap. He rocked my hips, fucking me slowly. I was completely on fire, burning up. He grabbed my chin and tilted until he could kiss me roughly, fiercely, almost swallowing me whole.

"You came for me just like I imagined," he said. "Hard and greedy. And beautiful." He rubbed his thumb over my lip. "So fucking beautiful."

Then he pushed me back onto the bed and began to fuck me as thoroughly as I hoped he would. There was nothing gentle about it, about him. The sounds he made, his balls slapping against my clit, the rough hold of his hands on my hips. He possessed me so fully I never wanted to come back. Will grabbed my hair and yanked it back, angling his hips so he hit my g-spot.

"Oh my *God*," I cried out, and Will sped up his rhythm, finally losing control. He flipped me over, pushed my legs open and pinned me beneath him. He grabbed my hands and held them over my head. With his other hand, he lifted my hips and slid back into me.

We both cried out. "I want to watch you come this time," he said, eyes focused in concentration.

"A... again?" I groaned, even though I was already racing back to the precipice. He angled me slightly higher, rocking against my clit.

"You'll come as many times as I tell you to," he said, biting my lip. It didn't take long. I unraveled beneath him, calling out hoarsely as a third orgasm tore through me. Will followed me over the edge, groaning my name over and over, mouth against my neck, his body shuddering.

We stayed like that for a long time, his cock still inside me, our hands bound together, panting. When he finally moved, my body mourned the loss. I heard him in the bathroom, rolling the condom off. I got a fine view of his ass and smiled, sighing with contentment.

When he came out, tender Will was back. He pulled me against him and kissed me gently. Sweetly. He cupped my face between his hands, then slid them down my body, tucking me even closer. He rubbed my ass, and I bit my lip at the slight discomfort.

"You won't be able to sit down tomorrow," his voice rumbled against my hair.

I smiled. "Good." He rubbed his hands over my body over and over, soothing. When he began massaging my scalp, I purred, drifting off.

"Violet..." I heard him say, but I knew what it was and didn't want to hear it. Couldn't.

I fell asleep instead.

9

WILL

*V*iolet slept like the angel I knew she wasn't. I watched her most of the night, keyed up and anxious. She was everything I dreamed her to be. More, even. I wanted to press "stop" on this night and suspend us here.

But I couldn't. We couldn't. So instead I watched her sleep and thought about what I would do. My dad was a detective. My grandfather was a beat cop.

Ten years.

Around dawn, I turned on my phone with a sick feeling in the pit of my stomach. There was a voicemail from the Sergeant. I brought it up to my ear and pressed play.

"Where the fuck are you, Will? I've been trying to call you for hours. Did someone kill you? Are you dead? I fucking hope not since you need to get that bitch into custody immediately. The victim that came in said he has her on a security camera, pointing a gun in his face and robbing him blind. We've got her, Will. We've got her."

I stopped the message before I could hear more. Violet shifted in her sleep, her dark hair fanning around her head. I moved over to the bed and sat up against the headboard, stroking the soft strands. My throat tightened.

Violet had gotten sloppy. I'd guessed guns were in the mix—you couldn't blackmail powerful people without a little bit of protection. But if she'd put it in the face of one of her marks, it meant she was desperate. Not a good sign.

She could get caught if she did it again.

If.

Violet opened her big blue eyes, and my heart stopped.

"Hi," she said sleepily and grinned like the Cheshire cat. I couldn't help but smile back.

"Good morning," I said, stroking her hair. She looked at me for a long time, and I held her gaze. I watched as the night came back to her—the pleasure, her fear, the arrest. Finally, her eyes landed on the badge and handcuffs I'd left on the nightstand.

"We should talk," I said.

Violet nodded and got up to use the bathroom, saying nothing. There were red welts all over her ass.

I stayed on the bed, staring at my hands.

She walked back over to me when she was done, sun glinting off the gorgeous curves of her body. Her hair was wild around her head, makeup smudged. I grew hard instantly. She crawled towards me across the bed with a condom in her hand. My mouth went dry.

"Violet..." I started, but there was no warning in it. Violet ran her tongue around the crown of my cock and down the shaft. And then she took me completely in her mouth.

My head fell back in total pleasure, hands in her hair. "You're going to be the death of me," I groaned, and a small smile tugged at her lips. Her eyes were closed in contentment as she sucked me deeper, the back of her throat beckoning.

I traced my fingers up and down her spine and over her perfect ass. I pushed two fingers into her pussy, and she moaned around my cock. I crooked my fingers, hitting the spot she liked. After a few minutes of complete bliss, I pulled her head up and pressed a hard kiss against her lips. "I need you," I said, and she responded by rolling the condom on with practiced skill. She straddled me with ease.

There were fingerprint-sized bruises around her hips, marks on her neck. "I'm sorry," I said, even though I wanted to mark her. Even though the sight of them made me want to bury my cock in her over and over again.

She shook her head, kissed me softly. "I like it," she said, then slid herself down the length of me.

The shock hit us both. She smiled, delighted, taking back a little bit of the control I'd stolen from her last night. She rocked against me, hands wrapped around my neck, face against mine. The blue of her eyes was startling.

We kissed for a long time, fucking slowly. I wanted it to last. Her nipples tasted like heaven in my mouth. Her hands tangled in my hair as I stroked the swell of her hips. I pulled my knees up so she could lean back and ride me like she wanted to, smiling, sighing, her clit swelling under my thumb. Her orgasm hit her sharply, and she cried out, taking me with her.

She pitched forward, and I wrapped my arms around her, nuzzling her hair. Violet's soft, sweet edges were just as tantalizing as her hard ones.

I heard something against my ear.

"What?" I asked.

"Sophie."

She leaned back, staring into my eyes. "My real name. It's Sophie."

Her trust.

"I never met my dad. He left... he left right before I was born. My mother loved him though, even after..." She trailed off for a second. "Even after all the other men she brought home, she still loved my dad best. Sophie was his mother's name, my grandmother."

I nodded, feeling like something was lodged in my throat. I had that feeling of my life branching out in front of me, of medals and awards and paperwork and the heavy, unending pressure of my entire existence.

I shifted Violet—Sophie—off me and onto the bed. "You have to run."

Her face looked quizzical for a second, then realization dawned on her.

"Why? You don't really have..."

I was suddenly frantic, fearful that I couldn't save her in time. "You have to run, now. Dye your hair, change your name, use only cash."

Her eyes flared, defiant as ever. "I know how to stay hidden."

I gripped her face between my hands. "I know you know how, gorgeous. I know. But I just got a call from my boss. They have you on that tape. Your face. The gun. It's over."

She shook her head. "No... Christopher? I thought..."

"You fucked up. And they want me to bring you in immediately. As in yesterday. Head somewhere else. Lay low for a while. For God's sake, don't blackmail anyone. Just... you need to go."

"Will... I..."

I stood, suddenly claustrophobic. "Vi—Sophie, you have to. I'll tell them you outsmarted me, that I lost my trail somehow."

I grabbed her clothing, her ripped shirt. I pulled one of mine from my suitcase and tossed it to her.

"Here, take this. And take my car too."

"What, and add even more to my record?" she said, hands on her hips.

I gave her an exasperated look, and she shrugged. "Fine, whatever, I'll take your car." She strapped on her stilettos and yanked on her skirt. I threw her a white undershirt, and she pulled it over her head.

Her nipples stood out stark against the transparent material. I wiped a hand over my mouth.

"Will," she said, and I saw a similar heat in her eyes.

"You have to go. *Now*," I said, throwing the car keys at her.

My phone rang, and we both knew who it was. I ignored it, pulling the door open and letting in the harsh light of the morning. "Do you need to get your stuff from your apartment?"

She shook her head. "No... oh shit, my laptop though. And the cameras."

So that was how she did it.

"Give me your keys. I'll destroy it. I promise."

She handed me her apartment key with shaking fingers. I grabbed them and pressed them to my mouth.

She looked at the car, back at me. The phone went off again, and she bit her lip.

"Will... what's going to happen to you—" she started, and I dragged her body against mine, kissing her with every ounce of passion I had in my body. She moaned against my lips, her hands around my neck, every inch of her body stretched against me. If this were another life, I would have taken her against the door.

But it wasn't. So I pulled away, reluctantly, and pressed my lips against her forehead.

"Thank you," I heard her say. "Thank you."

I wanted to say so much more. Instead, all I said was, "Just go." And she did.

I watched her drive away, the look she gave me filled with so much yearning it broke my heart. Behind me came the sound of the phone ringing, again, the path of my life broken now by this brief moment of dishonor. But I'd be fine. I could go back to being Good Cop easily. Quickly.

The phone rang and rang, and I slid Sophie's key around my finger.

Time to go destroy some evidence.

10

WILL

"I don't understand," my boss, the sergeant, said. Or growled, really, since he looked like he wanted to hit me over the head with the chair I was sitting in. "She just... lost you?"

"Fuck, Sarge... I don't know. One second I had her. The next?"

"Just to be clear, I don't believe a goddamn word coming out of your mouth right now."

I shifted uncomfortably and glanced at my watch. It'd been only four hours, and I prayed she'd gotten far enough away already.

"You don't have to," I said, spreading my hands. "But I'm not lying. Have you *ever* known me to lie?" It felt like ten years of honor had led up to this—guaranteeing her safety.

That got him, a little. Detective Will Furey was an honest man. A good man. A good cop, really.

Back at my desk, I stared at the piles of paperwork, the endless fingerprinting. I slid my handcuffs off my belt and placed them on my desk. They glinted back, mocking. The feel of her skin, her bound wrists, her beautiful trust.

Cuffed

I didn't want to be good anymore.

EPILOGUE

I felt, before I saw, Will's gaze on my legs. So I crossed them once, twice, knowing I'd pay for it later. I'd chosen The Dress just for him.

I thought about tempting him further, but then my mark showed up. Seth was one of the biggest developers in New Orleans. As soon as he saw me, his entire face lit up. Obsessed? Very. I gave him a little wave, and he almost tripped over his feet.

Manipulated? Definitely.

It'd been about a month for this one. Luckily, he liked boring, vanilla sex that lasted maybe seven minutes, max. Will didn't mind, as long as he could watch. And I thought about him the entire time.

This mark was also considering running for the local city council, a small step in his plan to eventually become governor. Seth had married his (filthy rich) wife because her father had been governor too—a two-term, beloved one. He'd been working towards this goal his entire fucking life.

Blackmail? Easily.

I fingered the USB stick I held in my hand, no longer as

nervous as I used to be. Behind Seth's back, I finally spotted Will. I shifted in my seat, squirming beneath his gaze.

"How are you, sweetheart?" Seth said, sliding into the seat in front of me. I swallowed my instinct to cringe.

"Happy," I said simply.

He reached forward for my hands. "Why so happy?"

"Because I'm about to come into a huge sum of money."

He arched an eyebrow, amused. "Really? How so?"

I leaned forward, grinning slowly, and held up the USB stick.

"Well, *sweetheart*, I've been filming our little lovemaking sessions this entire time. And every... single... one is on this stick."

I watched the usual range of emotions—shock, surprise, then furious anger. It didn't take him long.

"What the *fuck*," he said, gripping my wrist tightly. From the corner of my eye, I saw Will start to move, but I shook my head almost imperceptibly. He stopped.

"That's extortion."

"Mmmm," I said, untangling my wrist gently. "I like the term blackmail, but that's just me."

He sat back, crossed his arms. "I don't believe a word out of your lying mouth. There could be absolutely nothing at all on that stick."

I laughed, taking a long sip of my water. "True. Or I could deliver this to your wife tonight."

His eyes narrowed, and then he stood. This was why I always chose a public place.

"You won't get away with this," he said before spinning on his heel and stalking out of the restaurant. So dramatic.

I waited for a second, allowing my heart rate to slow. Then I stood, following him, the USB stick still in my hand. I walked past Will's table and traced my fingers over his shoulder.

Outside, the balmy New Orleans air felt like a lover's touch. New York City had been great, but I'd only been comfortable with two cons before it felt too dangerous. Plus, this city just suited me.

The mark was right up ahead, and I caught up to him, giving him a little push into the alley. I'd chosen this restaurant very, very carefully.

"We're not done talking," I said, and he turned around, spitting on the ground.

"Fuck you," he said, but I already felt Will behind me.

"Is there a problem here?" As usual, his deep voice had me shivering.

"Not at all," I said smoothly. "I'm just having a little fight with my boyfriend."

"Yeah right," Seth said snidely. "And who the fuck are you?" he asked.

"Detective Sanders," Will said, extending his hand forward. He flashed his badge, his thumb covering up his name. The mark looked at it, grateful for his good luck.

But Will hadn't been a detective in a long time.

"Well, thank God for you, sir," he said, running his hand through his hair. "This bitch is trying to blackmail me, which is a *crime* last time I checked."

He spat at my feet again. I stepped away, gingerly.

"Hmmm," Will said, taking out his phone and typing into it. "What's the issue exactly?"

Seth's face reddened slightly. "She says she taped us having sex. That she's going to give it to my wife. Cheating's not a crime, you know," he said hurriedly.

Will nodded, looking distracted. Then his face brightened, and he flipped the phone around.

"This video, you mean?"

He stepped closer in disbelief. There, on Will's small

screen, were our two bodies moving together. That night I'd blindfolded Seth so Will could watch more easily from the window without being spotted.

My punishment that night was to be blindfolded and tied, spread-eagled, to the bed while Will licked my pussy mercilessly. "Come for me," he'd growled over and over again until I was spent after orgasm number five.

I shook my head, clearing the memory and focusing. "Wait, what the..." the mark said, looking back and forth between us. I took out my phone and typed into the website our hacker-friend had given us (for a small cut, of course).

"Bank login and password info please," I said, businesslike.

"No way," he said.

Will cheerfully typed away at his phone. "What's your wife's email address again? Oh yeah, gloriawrightsman at—"

"*Don't*," Seth said, and we both stopped, grinning at him like loons.

We waited while he contemplated the only decision he really had. If looks could kill, we would have both been dead minutes ago. Then he rattled off his password information to me.

I typed it in, mouth watering when I saw how much money he had in there. But we always stuck to half a million. It was safe.

"You'll see $500,000 transferred out of your checking account and into another one. This account will close and disappear ten minutes after we leave you tonight. There will be no record of the transaction. If you tell anyone about what happened here, we will send this video to your wife so fast your head will spin." Will stepped closer to the mark, looming over him. "Are we clear?"

I finished the transfer quickly. "Done," I said, and Will stepped back to me.

Seth looked dejected... and pissed. "You two," he said, pointing a finger and walking away, "are fucking *monsters*."

He turned and ran, and I mentally checked him off my list.

"Bye," I said, waving my fingers at him. Will caught my hand and yanked me against his body. He kissed me roughly. We wouldn't need much more, really. There was a little villa in the south of France we'd had our eye on for some time. Our hacker friend was working on some fake passports for us that would be done any day now.

Will envisioned us lazing those days away, drinking expensive wine and dozing in the sun. Kissing. Fucking.

I knew we'd probably get into *some* kind of trouble. Maybe art forgery...

Will nibbled on my lip, bringing me back.

"Nicely done," he murmured.

"You as well... *Detective*."

He grinned at me, a grin that promised many, many dark things.

"Let's go home, Sophie."

AUTHOR'S NOTE

In late 2016, when I was a new indie romance author, I began writing short-form erotica based on sexy pictures I found online. Joyce coined them #SexyShorts! Before my Facebook group (Kathryn Nolan's Hippie Chicks) I'd write them sporadically – but joyfully. They were a delight for me – a way to play around with different tropes and writing styles; to get swept away in hot sex and foreplay.

When I launched my Facebook group, they premiered every Monday. Some were inspired by pictures sent to me by readers or polls compiled by my group members. I wrote a long #SexyShort serial called 'The Suit' that became a full-length novel called STRICTLY PROFESSIONAL. And this kept happening – shorts were becoming serials, released over weeks, and I was developing full characters and plots completely by accident. *This* is why #SexyShorts are so fun – they're written purely for enjoyment with only my (dirty) imagination to lead the way.

Readers have always loved my #SexyShorts and *I* have loved writing them for you. Your zeal and enthusiasm for bite-sized erotica never ceases to brighten my day. You asked for an anthology of #SexyShorts and I have delivered!

So enjoy this collection of fourteen of my very favorite #SexyShorts. They're erotic, steamy, filthy and slightly over-the-top. But it wouldn't be a Kathryn Nolan story without a sweet HEA.

Yours in smut,

Kathryn

ACKNOWLEDGMENTS

For the many readers and friends who requested this anthology – I hope you enjoyed Volume 1!

For Jodi, Joyce and Julia – my friends, confidantes and favorite supporters. Thank you for everything. I can't believe this beautiful journey we've gone on together!

For the Hippie Chicks – my #SexyShort cheerleaders! Thank you for your zealous enthusiasm, hilarious gifs, real-time-photographic-responses (looking at you, Sonal), sexy comments and creative inspiration. From historical romance to filthy MMF stories, you are my champions and I cannot thank you enough!

For Faith, Bronwyn, Lucy, Tammy, Beth, Sonal, Kelsey, Claire, Pippa, Jessica, Steph and the many, many people who lift me up and support me every day. Thank you from the bottom of my heart.

Always for Rob – the handsomest husband around. You're the ultimate hero for me.

HANG OUT WITH KATHRYN!

Sign up for my newsletter and receive exclusive content, bonus scenes and more!

I've got a reader group on Facebook called **Kathryn Nolan's Hippie Chicks**. We're all about motivation, girl power, sexy short stories and empowerment! Come join us.

Let's be friends on
Website: authorkathrynnolan.com
Instagram at: kathrynnolanromance
Facebook at: KatNolanRomance
Follow me on BookBub
Follow me on Amazon

ABOUT KATHRYN

I'm an adventurous hippie chick that loves to write steamy romance. My specialty is slow-burn sexual tension with plenty of witty dialogue and tons of heart.

I started my writing career in elementary school, writing about *Star Wars* and *Harry Potter* and inventing love stories in my journals. And I blame my obsession with slow-burn on my similar obsession for The *X-Files*.

I'm a born-and-raised Philly girl, but left for Northern California right after college, where I met my adorably-bearded husband. After living there for eight years, we decided to embark on an epic, six-month road trip, traveling across the country with our little van, Van Morrison. Eighteen states and 17,000 miles later, we're back in my hometown of Philadelphia for a bit... but I know the next adventure is just around the corner.

When I'm not spending the (early) mornings writing steamy love scenes with a strong cup of coffee, you can find me outdoors -- hiking, camping, traveling, yoga-ing.

BOOKS BY KATHRYN

BOHEMIAN

LANDSLIDE

RIPTIDE

STRICTLY PROFESSIONAL

SEXY SHORTS

BEHIND THE VEIL

WILD OPEN HEARTS

Made in the USA
Las Vegas, NV
30 April 2023